Mary's Son

A Tale of Christmas

Darryl Nyznyk

Cross Dove Publishing, LLC
Redondo Beach, California

This book is a work of fiction. Names, characters, places and events are products of the author's imagination or are used fictitiously. Any resemblance to actual events, locations or persons, living or deceased, is purely coincidental. We assume no responsibility for errors, inaccuracies, omissions, or any inconsistency herein.

First printing 2010

ISBN 978-0-9656513-5-6
LCCN 2010921738

DEDICATION

To my wife, Loretta, and our daughters,
Laura, Sarah, Julia, and Hannah,
so they will always remember the truth;

To Kelly, Wendy, Kaitlin, Kendall, Jeana,
Alex, Meg, and Autumn, who joined our daughters
as the first to experience this tale; and

To all who wish to live the true peace
and wonder of Christmas.

~ *1* ~

J ared Roberts was a man—thirteen years old—but a
  man nevertheless. He reached manhood suddenly, three
months after his father disappeared. It wasn't a conscious
decision. It just kind of happened. While his mother, three
sisters, and baby brother prayed Joe would return, Jared realized he wouldn't.

Joe Roberts had left almost a year before—Christmas Eve
morning. He was going to pick up some "last minute things,"
but he never returned. He simply vanished.

By nightfall, Jared's mother, Mary, was frantic. Joe had
never gone off without telling her. Although she tried to hide
her fear from the kids, she couldn't. Soon they were all worried.

When Mary called the police, they didn't show much interest.

"Your husband's a grown man. He's only been gone a day,
hasn't he? Give it some time," they'd said. But by the end of

the Roberts' family's worst Christmas ever, the police had to agree something was wrong.

The day Jared became a man, he decided the reason his father wasn't coming back was because he was dead. Although no one had found a body, Jared knew that was the only answer. He figured nothing else could keep his dad away from the family.

"Responsibility, son," Joe always said to Jared. "We don't run from responsibility. We take it head on and stick together as a family. No one will take care of us, and we should never expect anyone to. We take care of ourselves."

Joe would never leave his family like so many other fathers from the Sink had left theirs. "The Sink" was the name even the residents of the slums of East Penford used when referring to their part of town. It was the lowest point, by elevation, and, everyone agreed, it was the area to which all the filth drained. None who lived outside the Sink dared venture within its borders, and most who lived inside spent their lives trying to escape. Joe Roberts dreamed of leaving the Sink; but the dream always included his family. Joe wouldn't leave without the family because he wasn't like the other fathers. He was proud, and he was strong. Most importantly, though, Joe was responsible. That's why Jared believed Joe was dead. He'd be with his family if he wasn't.

Jared took his father's instruction to heart; he stepped up

when his family needed it. He took a part-time job sweeping the factory floors at Stone Industries after school. That was the company for which his father had worked. The little money he earned helped Mary, who worked two jobs of her own while Jared's nine-year-old sister Amanda took care of the five-year-old twins and two-year-old Billy after school.

For the first several months Jared wore a brave face. His siblings cried and asked for "daddy," but Jared never did. He was tough, a street kid who could handle anything. He figured part of his job was to hold the others together and show them he could be strong for them. But something started to happen around Halloween.

Jared hated the work at the factory. It didn't pay much, not enough to make a difference anyway, and he began to realize he didn't like all this "responsibility" stuff if it meant long hours of school and work with only a few pennies to show for it. To make matters worse, he heard comments and noticed the looks from the others at the factory. While the looks had been there all along because, he figured, they felt sorry for him, whispered comments about his father took him back to the day, three days before his father disappeared, when he overheard his parents talking in hushed, urgent tones.

Jared peeked into the kitchen that day and was shocked to see his father crying. He pulled back sharply behind the wall and slumped to the floor. He barely heard his father explaining that he'd been fired from his job at Stone Industries. The words didn't mean much to Jared at the time, but now they meant everything.

Whether Joe was dead or he had done the unthinkable and left the family, Jared suddenly understood the reason. His father disappeared because the company at which he'd worked for ten years fired him less than one week before Christmas. The comments Jared was hearing were that Joe had been fired because he'd stolen from the company. Jared knew that wasn't true. He would have known it even if he hadn't heard his father's tearful denial because he knew his father. Joe Roberts would never steal...or would he...if the family really needed it?

The fact was that Stone Industries had ruined Jared's life. It chased his father away, made his mother work two jobs, and forced him into a never ending cycle of meaningless work that paid him nothing. The family was in need because of the wrong done to his father. It was a terrible need as Christmas approached again. Jared knew what he had to do, and he was angry enough to do it.

It was on a bitterly cold night less than a week before Christmas that he met the other members of his gang in the town's abandoned rail yard. They were meeting to finalize a plan Jared had been working on since Halloween. The thirteen-year-old man stood before the glassless window frame of the old depot and stared up the hill to the lights of Penford Heights.

OUTSIDE the depot a boy skittered amidst moonlit shadows of rusted railcars. At the ramshackle building the boy hesitated, glanced cautiously about the grounds, and slipped through the battered entry. Inside, wayward beams of moonlight illuminated the fire-ravaged remains of the once-thriving station. The boy spied two figures crouching in the darkness behind Jared, who was pointing to a large Christmas-lit house on the hill.

"That's it, guys...Jonas Stone's house," the boy heard Jared say as he slunk in and sat down next to the other two.

"Sorry I'm late," whispered the boy. Michael "M.J." Johnson was a short, skinny twelve-year-old who came by the nickname "M.J." because of his love of basketball and his dream to someday be like Michael Jordan. "My dad came home tonight. He's tearin' our place apart..." his voice trailed off to silence as Jared turned and stared hard at him through the gloom.

"We don't need excuses," Jared said. "You gotta be here if you wanna be part of us."

Jared's look withered M.J., but he held his head up and nodded. Jared turned his attention to the boy next to M.J. "What'd Hank say, Hammer?"

Hammer was Joey Rodriguez, a big, strong thirteen-year-old who fashioned himself the best baseball player in the world, next to Jared. Next to Hammer sat Roger "Burner" Claiborne, another skinny boy, taller than M.J. and the fastest runner of all, next to Jared, of course.

"The party's on the twenty-second," Hammer answered.

"How's he know that?" Jared asked.

Hammer smiled. "The maid. He got it from the maid. She's got the hots for him." M.J. and Burner started to giggle until they realized Jared wasn't laughing. "She's working at the party," Hammer finished after shoving M.J. and Burner.

"Did he give you a layout of the house?" Jared asked.

Hammer reached into his pocket and withdrew a folded paper. "Yeah...but he wants a cut. He says he'll get us if we stiff him."

"He'll get his cut. Let's see it," Jared said. He, Hammer, and Burner leaned in to view the plan in the moon's dim light. M.J. held back, fidgety and unsure.

"Hey...Jared...guys...I don't know. I don't know if this is such a good idea."

"Whatsa matter, M.J....scared?" jeered Burner.

"I'm not scared.... It doesn't seem right.... I mean, it's not ours," M.J. stammered angrily.

Burner and Hammer squawked like chickens. Jared pushed Burner and said, "Shut up, you guys." He turned to M.J., "Whose is it?"

"It's not ours," M.J. answered sheepishly. "My mom says we got to take care of ours and leave to others what's theirs."

"Yeah, M.J., and where's that gotten you? A father who's a drunk and hardly ever around and a life where you got nothin' and will never have anything." He chuckled, turned, and stepped slowly back to the window frame. His mind wandered for a moment. In his early years Jared had been one of the "lucky kids" in the Sink because he'd actually had a father at home. He had a father who worked and cared for his family, a father who was there. But that ended a year ago, and he was just like all the rest now.

Jared turned back to M.J. "You think doing the right thing will help you and your sisters get outta here." He laughed sadly. "No way, M.J. We'll be here forever unless we take what we need."

"That's not true, Jared. We're workin' hard to get outta here," M.J. said.

"You ever seen anyone leave other than by jail or just runnin' out on others?" Jared sneered bitterly. He leaned against the window frame and stared again at the lights on the hill.

"This is our life," he said angrily. "We got to make our own way. Like they do on the hill," he pointed. "And we've got to make them pay for what they've taken from us."

"They aren't stealin', Jared," M.J. offered.

Jared turned slowly, shaking his head, while Burner and Hammer sat quietly, not wanting to get in the way of what Jared was going to do to M.J.

"What do you think they're doing?" Jared asked. "They do whatever it takes, and they don't consider it stealing. Money's the only reason they get respect, so they get it however they can. They got the bucks, and we don't. We're going to even things out a bit."

Burner spoke up softly, "Maybe M.J.'s right. No one's been able to get close to one of the big houses before. They got cops...."

Jared turned sharply. "What's wrong with you guys? Don't you get it? This is our chance. We do this, something nobody else could do, and we're somethin' here. We're not the dirt under Jonas Stone's boots anymore like everyone else is. We won't have to work for him for slave wages, afraid of being fired. We could make our own way."

Jared stared at his friends. They bowed their heads, ashamed of their fears.

"They owe us!" he said angrily. "We've got to take it 'cause they sure aren't going to hand it over. We got no choice."

Hammer and Burner nodded and turned to M.J. The youngest of the group had no more words. He knew his mother was right, but these were his friends...his best friends...the friends who would be there for him when he needed them. His code of responsibility to them would not let him turn away. M.J. eyed each of them before he nodded and joined them.

- 2 -

The next morning, in the house on the hill above the rail yard, Sarah Stone woke and rubbed the sleep out of her eyes. She stretched lazily and glanced around her oversized bedroom. The eleven-year-old had a private bathroom and a walk-in closet the size of most bedrooms. She lay amid satin sheets and a plush goose down comforter on her queen-sized canopy bed, her long, curly hair strewn about her. Slowly, she pushed herself up onto her elbows and looked toward her window, where she saw streaks of rain. She frowned at the weather and immediately began to consider her options for the day.

"Anna," she called.

When there was no response, she called again, this time a little louder.

Again no response.

"Anna!" she finally shouted and leaned over to her bedstand to angrily press a call button.

Within seconds her door burst open, and Anna, a pretty, olive-skinned girl in her early twenties ran in, breathing hard.

"You are awake, Miss Sarah," Anna said, trying to smile.

"Yes. I want to get up, now," Sarah responded haughtily and threw off her covers.

"Shall I start a bath, Miss Sarah?"

"Yes, and get my blue denim outfit. I'm going to the mall today."

Anna raised her eyebrows, turned toward the bathroom, and smiled. She knew something Sarah had apparently forgotten, and she relished the thought of Sarah's bitter disappointment when the spoiled girl realized she wasn't going anywhere today. It wasn't that Anna was a mean person. She didn't like for people to be sad. It was simply that Sarah was such an obnoxious brat, who treated all the hired help so badly that some of them, Anna included, actually smiled when the young mistress suffered disappointment. Anna had heard the young girl hadn't always been this way. When her mother was alive, she had been such a pleasant child, some of the older help said. But that was long ago, and the only Sarah Anna knew was the current version; and she didn't like her very much.

"Is my father home?" Sarah asked. She was standing in front of her mirror, frowning, testing her look of superiority before she turned back to Anna.

"Yes, Miss Sarah."

"Good. Tell him I'd like him to take me to the mall today."

"He's in a meeting in his study, Miss Sarah. He said no one was to disturb him." Anna smiled as she turned to the girl's closet.

"But, it's Sunday...." Sarah pouted for a moment before she realized she was showing weakness. She turned again to Anna, who was making the bed and laying out the blue outfit.

"Well...then tell Brockton to have the car ready out front," Sarah rallied.

"Oh...did you forget, Miss Sarah? Mr. Brockton quit last night. He believed it was you who poured jalapeño sauce in his tea. He was very angry. Miss Grundick will look tomorrow for a new driver for you," Anna said before walking back to the bathroom.

Sarah turned to hide her disappointment. She hated the thought of being cooped up in the house all day.

Sarah had, indeed, sabotaged Brockton Smith's tea. It was just a joke. He should never have taken it so seriously. Anyway, she never cared all that much for Mr. Smith. He was always such a grouch. She smiled as she remembered the look on his face when he first tasted the extra-hot jalapeño in his tea. It was that look of bulging eyes set wide in his quickly reddening face, mottled by sudden drops of perspiration, that made the prank and her current predicament almost bearable. Sarah turned and walked slowly to her window, where she tried to think of something else to do on this rain-spattered day.

"Will that be all, Miss Sarah?"

"Yes...for now," she answered.

Sarah stared absently through the water rivulets, contemplating her ill fortune, when suddenly she caught sight of a plump little man standing on the sidewalk, outside the grounds of her home. He wore a dark suit and a round-top, narrow-brimmed bowler set high atop a shock of white hair. He clutched a small black case in one hand and seemed to have appeared out of nowhere.

The man stood in front of a granite-pillared, wrought-iron gate that guarded the Stone estate. The rain, now pouring, plastered his beard and the hair beneath the hat. He glanced up and squinted as if he was noticing for the first time that it was raining.

Sarah leaned closer to the glass to get a better look, but her breath fogged the pane. She rubbed the glass quickly and shifted position, only to find that the man now held a black umbrella above his head. At least she believed he held the umbrella because no other explanation for its existence came to her mind. The umbrella was open and suspended at the proper height to protect the man from the rain. It looked, however, as if he wasn't holding it—as if it really was just hanging above his head, until he finally seemed to reach out and grab the handle. But Sarah knew that couldn't be. He must have been holding it all along and had simply opened and lifted it above his head while she wiped the window. When the heavy gate began to swing open in front of him, even though he appeared to make no movement toward it, Sarah knew something strange was happening.

She followed the man's progress through the gate, up the driveway, and toward the front door, until she was sure he was coming to visit. She then jumped away from the window, ran to her closet to don her robe and slippers, and ran out the door. This visit was sure to occupy at least a part of her morning.

THE plump man stood a shade less than five feet five inches tall. His weight was something he never discussed, for he knew it was too much. His ruddy cheeks and button nose were framed by long white hair and a beard. His round face seemed always to be smiling. The man pushed his wire-rim glasses firmly onto the bridge of his nose as he found himself standing before two massive doors. He closed and leaned his umbrella against the door jamb, shook the water from himself, grabbed the heavy gold knocker, and struck the door twice.

Within a minute, one of the doors swung open, and the little man grinned cheerily at a tall, very thin man with sharp, hawk-like features. The tall man held his head very high, and the little man wondered how, with his head so high, the tall man could see him.

"May I help you?" the tall man asked with a proper English accent.

"Good day, Sir." The little man bowed slightly and reached to tip his hat, only to find that he no longer wore one. He turned quickly in search of the wayward derby on the walk and driveway behind him but saw nothing. He shrugged absently and turned back to the doorman.

"Yes!" the doorman said expectantly, distaste clearly etched on his face.

"Good day, Sir," the little man started again with a broad smile. "My name is Nicholas. I understand that you are looking for someone to care for the child of the house."

The doorman dropped his head slightly to stare down his beak nose and get a better look at Nicholas. His eyes worked their way down to Nicholas's feet, where he stopped suddenly and frowned at the sight of the little man's white tennis shoes.

"They're really quite comfortable," Nicholas said.

"One moment." The doorman was clearly unimpressed. He swung the door shut and turned away. Before the door could close, Nicholas jammed the tip of his umbrella between the door and its threshold. He pushed the door open slowly and walked into the great hall, his shoes squeaking on the polished marble floor.

"This is quite a place," Nicholas whispered to himself.

His shoes continued to squeak loudly as he made his way around the hall. So large was the foyer that he finally had to stop and view its overwhelming wonder from where he stood. His eyes took in all the grand beauty until they finally landed at the top of the magnificent staircase, where Sarah was standing, staring at him. He smiled and waved.

"Well, good morning…Sarah, isn't it? Sarah Stone?"

Sarah stared, dumbfounded, first because the plump man knew her name and second because he wore black, hard-soled oxford shoes on his feet. She could have sworn he'd entered the house with white tennis shoes that squeaked when he walked, yet now his shoes weren't white, and they certainly weren't tennis shoes. Before Sarah could gather her wits and say something, the doorman returned to the foyer.

"Come this way," the doorman instructed.

Nicholas winked at Sarah and followed the doorman into a large room lined with dark mahogany floor-to-ceiling shelves stacked neatly with books. At the far side of the room, which Nicholas deduced was the library, was a large L-shaped black leather couch that surrounded a low-standing mahogany coffee table with several over-sized volumes splayed across its top. In the two near corners of the room were writing tables of the same dark wood, each accompanied by two ornately carved chairs with cushions covered in dark velvet on the seats. The doorman ushered Nicholas to one of the writing tables, handed him a form and pen, and motioned him to take a seat. Nicholas obliged the man with a cheery smile.

"Fill this out before Miss Grundick arrives," the doorman instructed.

"Yes...thank you, Mr....er.... What is your name, my good man?"

"Stevens," he responded haughtily.

"Stevens...oh, yes, Stevens, thank you." Stevens turned to leave when Nicholas suddenly remembered something. "Oh...Stevens," he said, "You're not Jonathan Stevens of Yorkshire, are you?"

Stevens turned abruptly, shocked by Nicholas's innocent question.

Nicholas continued, "Ah...I knew it. Do you remember as a boy when you always wanted to leave crumb cakes for Santa instead of cookies?"

Stevens brightened. "Why, yes. How..." he started.

"That was a good choice, my boy. Really quite tasty," Nicholas interrupted and patted his ample belly.

"Did you really like..." Stevens forgot himself for an instant before his smile disappeared again and he returned to his former demeanor. "Yes...well, Miss Grundick will be here shortly," he said. "You'd better complete the form."

"Yes...of course. Well, we'll talk later...Jonathan. Thank you."

Stevens turned sharply and scurried out of the room.

SARAH dressed quickly. All thoughts of a morning bath disappeared. She threw on the blue denim and tried to brush through her tangled curls before she gave up and tied her mass of hair in a ponytail.

Sarah had been to circus acts and "magic parties." As a very young girl, she loved those events. But her mother's death ended her fascination with magic. The car accident that took her mother also took the magic out of her life. By the time she'd reached her eleventh birthday, not only did she not believe in magic, she was actually able to explain how magic tricks were done. She could no longer be fooled, even for a moment...at least until this very morning when the plump little man appeared at her gate.

Sarah's mind told her the man had been carrying the umbrella from the first moment she'd seen him. How else could he have been completely dry when he entered the house? As for the shoes, she'd simply been mistaken the first time she saw him. He'd worn the hard-soled oxfords the entire time. Yet Sarah's interest was piqued. She had to find out who this little man was.

MYRA Grundick entered the library as Nicholas was completing the form. She was a thin, sharp-edged woman with dark hair pulled back tightly, uncomfortable in the tension it brought to her face, which despite the pull appeared pinched as if it was in a constant battle with the tightness of the hair. She was stiff, cold, businesslike and unsmiling. Upon her entry, Nicholas stood and extended his hand in greeting.

"Good morning, Miss...Grundick, I believe. Myra Grundick, is it?"

"May we help you?" she asked. Her face pinched even more as she stared disdainfully at Nicholas. She did not take his hand. Although he continued to smile, Nicholas withdrew his, a little puzzled.

"Actually, I thought perhaps I could help you, Miss. I understand you need a man to help care for the little girl of the house. I've filled out your form," he said, and handed it to her.

"How did you know of our need? I've only just prepared the notice to go to the agencies tomorrow." She took a folded paper from her dress pocket and held it up for Nicholas to see. His smile faded.

"Yes...well..." Nicholas stammered for a second before he again smiled broadly. "Well, your man, Brockton Smith, quit last night. I learned of your need as a result of his departure. Apparently the girl is quite a handful. Spirited you might say."

Myra Grundick frowned as she began to review the application. "Well, Mr....er, Mr. Nicholas.... What is your first name?"

"That's it. You've said it...only the 'Mr.' is not really necessary."

"What is your last name, then?"

"I was afraid you'd ask that. You see, I haven't used it in so many years, I've really quite forgotten it," Nicholas frowned. His voice trailed off.

Myra Grundick didn't hear his last statement because she was shocked by the rest of the information she read. Nicholas spoke quickly and tried to distract her from the form.

"I've had many years of experience with children. I'm really quite good with them."

"Is this some kind of a joke?" she demanded.

"Joke?... Why, no. I am here to help you care for the girl."

"You say here that you are also known by the names Kris Kringle...and Santa Claus?" She stared hard at him and drew out the last words with a slow, angry exhalation.

"It is the truth, Miss Grundick. All of it. I am..." Nicholas stammered.

Miss Grundick turned to Stevens, who was standing at the library's entry.

"Stevens, show this man out," she commanded.

"Yes, Miss. This way," Stevens said as he strode into the room and took Nicholas's arm.

Nicholas chastised himself silently. He wondered if he would ever learn. This seemed to happen every time he filled out one of those forms or tried to explain his history to someone. They never believed him, yet he never learned. Part of it was that he could not lie...it was a part of his very being that he could only speak the truth. Perhaps it would have been better if he'd simply refused to fill out the form.

Nicholas frowned as Stevens led him through the library doorway. He glanced up at the taller man and then sadly over his shoulder at an angry Myra Grundick. When the woman turned sharply to walk away, Nicholas called out to her.

"Myra...you really should smile, my dear. You had such a pretty smile as a child," he said, hoping to touch a nerve. And he did. She turned on him.

"Leave this house immediately!" she shouted. "Don't waste our time any longer!"

When Stevens and Nicholas entered the foyer, Sarah came bounding down the stairs.

"Where are you going?" she asked Nicholas. Then, before he could respond, she turned to Stevens. "Where are you taking him?"

"I'm showing him out, Miss Sarah."

"No!" she shouted and ran to the door, where she spread her arms to block their path. "I don't want him to go.... Stop!"

"Miss Grundick ordered him out," Stevens explained.

"I don't care! I want him to stay!" Sarah's voice grew louder.

"But, Miss Sarah, I don't understand."

"I want him to stay here. Leave him!" Sarah continued.

"Sarah! Stop this foolishness!" Miss Grundick commanded when she entered the hall. "This man will not stay in this house!"

At first, Sarah was taken aback by Miss Grundick's sudden appearance, but she recovered quickly. She turned on the lady with an even louder shrill cry.

"Yes, he will! I want him to stay!"

Sarah ran to Nicholas's side and grabbed his free arm. Miss Grundick stepped toward Sarah with a look on her face near rage. She grabbed the girl, who now clung tightly to Nicholas. Nicholas leaned toward Stevens for balance as Miss Grundick tugged at Sarah. The girl screamed. Nicholas and Stevens cringed from the ear-splitting sound. Miss Grundick pulled and tugged with more urgency, and Sarah, wrapping her legs around Nicholas's leg, screamed even louder.

At the far end of the foyer, a door suddenly burst open. A tall, athletically built man stormed through. He was in his early forties, with dark hair graying slightly at the temples, distinguished looking in every way that enormous wealth could buy. Everyone turned to him; silence suddenly reigned. Jonas Stone, Sarah's father, stared at the scene, Stevens holding one of Nicholas's arms, Sarah clinging to the other, and Miss Grundick trying to dislodge Sarah.

"What's going on here?" he demanded as he strode angrily toward them.

Miss Grundick, Sarah, and Stevens spoke at the same instant as Nicholas stood placidly, looking the part of a reasonable man being put upon by three unreasonable people.

"This man is a fraud, Sir, who..." Miss Grundick started.

"I'm trying to show this man to the..." said Stevens.

"I want him to stay, Daddy.... I want..." Sarah begged.

Jonas Stone stopped his advance about ten feet away from them, dropped his head, and held up both hands for silence.

"Miss Grundick, I am trying to conduct a very important meeting. You are here to maintain order so I can concentrate on my business affairs. Can't you take care of an eleven-year old girl?"

"Of course, Sir," she responded testily, releasing Sarah and standing upright.

"Then please do so," Jonas instructed as he stared hard from one face to the other, before he turned back sharply toward his office.

Sarah's chance of winning the day faded with each step Jonas took toward the office; but she'd been in this situation before. Her father was so busy, he didn't have time to deal with anything other than his meeting. She knew how to handle these scenes because she'd done it so often over the years.

"Daddy!" she shouted before Jonas could regain the safety of his office. "Don't let them send him away!"

"Sarah! Your father is busy. Now...." Ms. Grundick again pulled at Sarah, who was still clinging to Nicholas.

"No, I won't let go! I won't be quiet until you say he can stay."

Jonas Stone whirled around and marched back to the

group. He searched their faces for some sanity. "Stevens, what's going on here?" he finally demanded.

"This gentleman came here to apply for the position that was left open by Mr. Smith's untimely...retirement, Sir. I was showing him to the door when Miss Sarah stepped in to prevent his departure," Stevens explained quickly.

Jonas glanced at a smiling Nicholas as his daughter clung tightly to the man's arm and leg. She stared at him pleadingly. He shrugged.

"What's the problem, Miss Grundick?" he asked, recognizing that the only way he'd complete his meeting was to satisfy his daughter.

Miss Grundick released Sarah again, stood, and regained her composure. "He says one of his names is Santa Claus, Sir," she said with a look of triumph.

Even Sarah was stunned by that revelation. She loosened her grip on Nicholas for an instant, stared up at him, and then resolved that the new fact only made things that much more interesting.

Jonas smiled. "Well, he certainly looks the part, doesn't he? He seems harmless enough."

"He has no references, Mr. Stone. We must look into his history," Miss Grundick stammered, stunned at Jonas's carelessness.

"Well, Mr...." Jonas turned to Nicholas.

"Nicholas, Sir."

"Well, Mr. Nicholas, have you ever worked with children before?"

"Oh, yes—for many years. Working with children has been my life."

Jonas glanced at his daughter, who continued to cling to Nicholas. He looked again at Nicholas's round, smiling, cherry-cheeked face and sparkling blue eyes before he turned to Miss Grundick.

"Miss Grundick, come with me, please."

When they were out of earshot of the others, Jonas whispered, "I see no reason why he can't stay for the day."

"But, Sir," she protested, "we know nothing about the man. He could be anything at all."

"He'll keep Sarah quiet today. That's what I need. I cannot have any further interruptions."

"But, Sir..." the lady tried again.

"He will stay today, Miss Grundick," Jonas commanded. "Have Stevens drive Sarah and this Mr. Nicholas to the mall. Make sure Stevens stays with them at all times. He can sleep in the guest quarters tonight. Tomorrow, we'll talk further about him.... Now, I must get back to work."

~ 3 ~

Heavy black clouds dumped torrents of rain on the pock-marked streets of the Sink. The once thriving Main Street business area of town was devastated. Except for the few pawnshops, an iron-barred market, two all-night liquor stores, three bars, and a Goodwill store, the dreary, gray buildings were boarded up, gutted, and in a state of complete deterioration. Homeless people huddled amid scavenged blankets in the few doorways, which provided a semblance of protection from the rain.

Off Main Street, the ramshackle residences of the Sink described a haphazard patchwork of disintegrating corrugated metal roofs, crumbling chimneys, leaking window frames, and heating and electrical systems that worked only when they weren't needed.

It was in one of these residences, albeit somewhat better kept than most, that Mary Roberts stood in front of an old gas range, mixing a small pot of oatmeal. Mary was thirty-five years old and still pretty despite her hardships over the past year. She smiled through tired eyes and tried her best every day to look past the poverty surrounding her.

It wasn't really that long ago that her family had actually laughed together despite hard times. They had laughed with the knowledge that things would one day be better. Although it seemed an eternity since Joe's disappearance, it had been only a year—a period of anguish and fear for Mary and of loss and abandonment for her children. Although the youngest children were spared Mary's personal pain as she worked hard at maintaining the fiction that their father would "be home soon," it was upon the older two that Mary unintentionally leaned for support. Even with them she tried to be strong, but Amanda and Jared knew better. They had seen the changes in their mother. They witnessed the swollen red eyes in the morning, the downward turn at the sad corners of her mouth, and the droop in the shoulders of the once strong woman.

Now, as another Christmas approached without any word of Joe, Mary had given up hope he'd ever return. She had resigned herself to raising her five children alone. Like so many other families in the community, hers was without a husband and a father for her children. She needed to be strong to provide her young charges with hope.

"Come on, kids," she called. She tried to be cheery but

knew her voice sounded heavy. "We've got to eat now, or we'll be late."

She spooned the steaming oatmeal into six bowls and placed them on the table. Within seconds Amanda bustled into the kitchen, carrying her fidgeting brother, Billy. Both kids wore their best clothes, frayed and a bit tattered but clean and as pressed as possible given the kids' age and rambunctiousness.

"How do we look, Momma?" asked Amanda.

"Beautiful, honey." She smiled at her daughter and took Billy. "And you're so handsome," she cooed at the boy. "I'll feed Billy, Amanda. You get your sisters and Jared, okay? We don't want to be late for services."

Amanda returned within minutes with Kayla and Katie in tow. Although they were twins, the only resemblance between the two was in their black hair worn in tightly braided pigtails. Kayla was lean and quick, a half head taller than Katie. Katie was a good ten pounds heavier than her twin, and her gait was slow and deliberate.

The three girls took their places around the table.

"Well, you two look pretty," Mary said to the twins. "Where's Jared?"

"He's still in bed, Momma," offered Katie.

"He said he'll be down soon," said Amanda.

"Well, we'll have to start without him," said Mary.

They bowed their heads and began to say grace together as Billy smiled and pounded on his high-chair tray. After the prayer, Mary poured milk into the bowls and passed them around the table. When Jared walked in, still disheveled from sleep and sporting a sour look, Mary smiled at him but said nothing.

"Can we go see Santa today, Momma?" asked Kayla.

"Maybe after church, honey. C'mon now, eat quickly because it's almost time to go." She glanced at Jared and asked, "Aren't you coming with us, Jared?"

"Naw. I've got to see the guys this morning," he grunted at her, stretched, glanced at the oatmeal, and frowned.

"Can't you see them after services?" Mary asked.

"Momma, do you think Santa can bring me a bike this year?" interrupted Amanda.

Mary turned slowly from Jared, who rolled his eyes at the stupidity of his sister's question.

"You can ask him, child. We'll see," Mary answered.

"C'mon, Amanda. You're too old to believe in Santa," Jared blurted.

All sound at the table ceased. The three girls stared at their brother. Mary's eyebrows raised in a plea for Jared to hush.

"Well...she is," Jared continued. "There's no real Santa, so why even...."

"Yes there is!" shouted the twins.

"Jared! That's enough!" exclaimed Mary.

"Well, why fill them with false hope, Mom?" he asked, angrily. "This is all we'll ever have. Why dream?"

"Jared! Stop that talk!" Mary almost shouted.

"Jared's wrong, isn't he, Momma?" asked Katie.

Mary glared at Jared. "Of course he's wrong, honey. For those who don't believe in Santa, he never comes. If you believe, he'll do wonderful things for you."

Despite the family's perilous financial condition, Mary wanted desperately to help her kids maintain at least some sense of fantasy in their lives, if only for a little while longer, before they too had to deal with the harsh realities of life. She worked every day as a secretary at Stone Industries. And even though her supervisor had apologized on behalf of the company for firing Joe when they'd found the real thief, it hadn't brought Joe back, and she was angry. But she'd had no choice but to keep the job as well as find a part-time night job at a mall card shop. Every cent helped, especially at Christmas. She again stared at Jared, trying with her eyes to make him stop spreading his bitterness.

Jared pushed his bowl away and stood up abruptly as the twins turned at him with a "see, I told you so" look. Amanda continued to stare at her mother, doubt suddenly creeping into her mind. Mary turned back to Amanda.

"We'll go see him today." Then to Jared, "Where are you going?"

"Out!"

Jared grabbed his sweatshirt and opened the door. Mary jumped out of her own seat to follow him. "Amanda, keep an eye on Billy for a minute," she said.

"Jared," she called when she reached the door and saw her son start to run. "Jared, please wait a minute."

Although the rain had stopped, it was still gray, dreary, and promising more. Jared, ashamed, bewildered, and angry, turned slowly.

"Don't do this to yourself," Mary pleaded. "And please don't do this to your sisters. Don't make them feel there's no hope."

"Well, there isn't, Ma. What's to hope for? We're poor; we'll never get outta here."

"Don't ever say that again," she flared. "We don't have money, but we've got each other. We need to stick together and help each other. If we do, God will always be there for us."

"Ah, Mom, what's God done for us?"

"You're healthy. And he's given us all the ability to help ourselves."

"How can you say that, Mom? We got nothin'."

"You can't lose hope or...." She hesitated as tears came to her eyes. She had meant to mention Joe, but she couldn't.

The pain was almost unbearable. After a few seconds she regathered her strength and continued. "I want this family to stick together, Jared. We need you."

Jared dropped his head. "I won't leave you. Don't worry about that." He hesitated, not sure whether to go back to his mother or keep moving. Finally, he shrugged toward the street and said resignedly, "Look, I gotta go. The guys are waiting."

"I love you," Mary said as Jared turned away. She understood the burdens her young son carried. He was the man of the house and took the responsibility seriously. It weighed heavily on him, and Mary felt so bad that such a young man had to carry such a load.

Jared disappeared at a run as he whispered, "I love you too, Mom."

"I DON'T trust him, Mr. Stevens," whispered Myra Grundick. She gave Stevens final instructions for the day's outing. "Watch him closely and report everything to me. I want him out of here by tomorrow morning."

Stevens nodded conspiratorially and marched determinedly out of the house.

Outside, the gray dreariness was finally giving way to

bright greens and soft blues as streaks of sunlight began to push their way through the clouds. Wet pavement and leaves bearing drops of rain sparkled in the sun's expanding rays. Stevens opened the back door of a large white Mercedes. Sarah was dressed in a long brown coat with fox fur cuffs and collar. She marched smartly down the front steps and into the car's backseat.

Nicholas came after Sarah. He walked nonchalantly with his hands clasped loosely behind his back and his eyes scanning the beauty of the rain-washed world around him. When he reached the car's back door, held open for him by Stevens, he turned his smile toward the man.

"Beautiful day, isn't it, Jonathan? Much like home for you," he said.

Stevens held his head high, trying to ignore the comment but found himself wanting to answer the unusual little man. He couldn't help thinking that Nicholas seemed to be such a happy, harmless fellow. Yet, in this day, those types could prove to be the worst of all. "You could never know for sure," he said to himself as he shut the door and moved around to assume his position behind the wheel.

After Sarah fastened her seatbelt, she watched with some curiosity as Nicholas fumbled with his; but after several seconds, the curiosity was gone. She became exasperated and reached over to fasten his belt.

"Thank you, Sarah. You know, I never have learned to operate one of these automobiles. Or for that matter any of the belts and things inside." Nicholas turned forward as the car began moving. "Wonderful invention—much nicer than they used to be."

Nicholas nodded once at Sarah and then turned contentedly to his window to watch the world zip past him. Soon, however, he felt Sarah's gaze boring into him, and he turned to her with his ever-present smile.

"Where were you hiding it?" she asked.

"What's that, my dear?"

"The umbrella, of course. And how did you change the shoes?"

"Oh, you saw that, did you?" Sarah nodded slowly and stared intently at the man, hoping to discern the magician's lie she was expecting. "Well, Sarah," he continued, "I really didn't do any of that...Peter did."

The girl sat back with a quizzical look. That was an answer she hadn't expected. Normally magicians conjured stories to embellish their tricks, but this man was taking a different approach. It was an imaginary friend named Peter who had helped him. This could be interesting, Sarah thought.

"Who's Peter?" she asked.

Stevens pressed back into his seat to hear the response.

Nicholas hesitated and thought carefully before he answered the girl.

"Well, it wasn't actually Peter who did it...you see, I told Peter we'd forgotten something...and suddenly...the umbrella was there in front of me and I...had new shoes."

Stevens smiled broadly at that comment. In his rearview mirror he saw Sarah's eyes narrow. He knew the girl wouldn't believe something so outlandish.

The girl eyed Nicholas in silence, trying to make sense of what she had just heard. She had long ago given up all her imaginary friends. Yet, sitting next to her was this unusual man who spoke of an imaginary friend as if he was real. This was an area of adult behavior Sarah had never seen except in movies involving crazy people. But this was real. Nicholas was actually sitting next to her, and she didn't know how to react. Instead, she decided to change her tack.

"Who are you, Nicholas?" she asked.

"You've said it, my dear. I'm Nicholas. Unfortunately, though, I can't remember my last name. It's been so long since I've used it.... You and most children would know me as Santa Claus."

This time Stevens' eyes grew wide, and he swerved the car with a quick pull of the wheel. Despite Nicholas's written claim in the application and his seeming knowledge of things about Stevens' youth only a "Santa Claus" would know, it hadn't really struck Stevens that the man truly thought he was Santa Claus. Yet it now appeared he did.

Sarah didn't hesitate for a moment. "No, you're not!" she said flatly. "I heard what Miss Grundick said. I want you to tell me the truth. You are not Santa Claus," she concluded.

"Oh, yes...I am. Why do you say I'm not?"

Sarah's anger turned to haughtiness. If there was one thing she knew for a fact it was that there was no such thing, and she really needed to get past this issue quickly.

"Because Santa Claus doesn't exist," she responded. "Everyone with any brains knows that."

"I certainly hope there aren't many people with any brains then, because I wouldn't have many believing in me," Nicholas retorted.

"There's no such thing as Santa Claus!" Sarah said firmly. "You're lying!" She turned away from Nicholas.

Nicholas's smile faded. It was not unusual for eleven-year olds to stop believing in Santa. Although that bothered him, Nicholas's real concern was with the extreme intensity of Sarah's feeling.

"Of course there is, Sarah, and I'm him," Nicholas said. "But for those who don't believe in me, I can't exist. I can help only those who believe. Why do you feel I don't exist?"

"You don't...I mean you do.... But...you're not Santa Claus. There's no such person." Sarah was flustered. She turned again and stared out her window, arms folded in front of her, angry. While Nicholas frowned sadly, Stevens tried to smile, knowing Nicholas had sealed his fate in the Stone employ. It was clear Sarah had nothing more to discuss with Nicholas. Stevens should have been happy that the little man—whatever his purpose—had destroyed any chance of prolonging his stay with the Stones. But, for some reason, he was not. The intensity of Sarah's feeling on the subject surprised him. He had always loved Christmas and the hopes and wonders it brought to his youth. To see that Sarah, at such a young age, had none of those hopes made him feel some of the same sadness Nicholas's face showed.

$\sim 4 \sim$

For Sarah, the mall was an escape. Living in a mansion as an only child surrounded by servants, cooks, maintenance workers, maids, and other adults intent on their household tasks left Sarah without any real human companionship. Because she went to a private school some distance from her home, she had no friends within easy access, and if the truth were told, even those at school with whom she had contact were not really friends at all. The occasional help like Brockton Smith, who was hired to keep her out of everyone else's hair, provided her no friendship. The Brockton Smiths of her world weren't there to listen to her problems or to advise her how one might deal with an issue or even join her in some fun activity. They were there simply to watch over her, make sure she was safe, discipline her where necessary, and always report the day's events to Miss Grundick so she could assure Sarah's father that Sarah was indeed active each day.

Sarah loved her father, although not the way she did when she was little, of course. Then, she adored him. Now, she was too old for that. Jonas was her father, and she loved him the way all kids were supposed to love their fathers. If she gave the matter any thought, she figured her love changed because that was what happened when kids got older. After all, he changed, didn't he? He was different than when she was younger. Back when her mother, Annie, was still alive, he was happy—fun too. He always wanted to hang out with Sarah and Annie. He liked that even more than work it seemed.

When the drunk driver crossed into Annie's lane and caused the collision that killed both drivers, Sarah was five years old. She remembered her daddy, as she called him at the time, crying a lot after that. She cried with him because mommy wasn't coming home anymore, and even though she didn't understand everything that happened, she did understand that her daddy was very sad. She tried to make him happy with hugs as much as she could, but soon she began to see him a lot less. He became busier at work, and Sarah grew into her own world of private school and escorts by hired help. She and her father spent less time together, and every day there seemed to be fewer hugs, until, one day, there were none.

Jonas was still Sarah's father. He made sure she was cared for and that she had the best education and the best clothes and the best electronics. As Sarah grew older, she learned to accept the changes in him. She'd throw tantrums, of course.

What kid didn't? And she'd do whatever was needed to get her way. As she got older, she also learned about the world. She learned it didn't care. No one really did, and if she wanted attention, as everyone did from time to time, she would simply have to demand it. Demanding attention was something at which she became very good.

At home she got attention when she was tedious or troublesome. But that attention was a reaction and had no real meaning. She learned quickly that the only time the attention given her was even partially genuine was when she was on an outing. At home, the attention was simply to keep her quiet and out of everyone's way as they all went about their daily business. It was only on outings specifically intended for her that she was totally in control. That's why the mall was her escape. Whoever took her to the mall had only one purpose...to accompany Sarah and to focus on her the entire time. At the mall, she was in charge, and whoever was with her had nothing else that he needed to do—that is, until Nicholas came along.

On this day, Sarah led Stevens and Nicholas through the labyrinth of shops. Stevens was his usual, attentive self, but Nicholas didn't seem to understand his place. He ambled amidst Christmas shoppers, his hands clasped behind his back and his eyes sparkling in the bright decorations. He was preoccupied with the noise, bustle, and craziness of the season's shopping, and he showed little interest in Sarah's needs as he trailed her and Stevens by large distances.

"Mr. Stevens," Sarah finally demanded, "will you tell Nicholas to join us?"

Sarah had to admit, as she waited for Stevens to catch Nicholas's eye, that he bore a striking resemblance to the impish symbol of Christmas. He wandered aimlessly through the crowd, greeting everyone with bright smiles and jolly calls of "Merry Christmas." Maybe it was because he looked like Santa that he thought he was Santa.

"Whatever," she thought. It didn't matter right now anyway. This was her time, and he was supposed to be with her. He was supposed to be helping her find what she wanted, noting her choices and then having them wrapped and delivered to her house. He wasn't supposed to be wandering around, greeting other kids and smiling at everyone he passed.

Stevens craned his neck and waved embarrassingly until Nicholas finally saw him. Nicholas smiled, nodded cheerily, and stepped up his pace. Sarah turned sharply into the nearest store, a Fitzpatrick & Ames teeming with swaggering teens and parents shocked by the half-naked live models as well as the prices of the few stitches of clothing they wore.

When Nicholas finally joined Stevens at the store, he didn't enter. Instead, he took Stevens by the arm and whispered to him.

"She doesn't need me in there, Jonathan. I'll wait out here for you."

"No, Mr. Nicholas, I'm sure she wants you inside the store. You'd better come in," Stevens said.

Nicholas shook his head and patted Stevens on the arm as he looked past him and saw Sarah. She was moving purposefully, oblivious to all except whatever shopping mission she was on.

"We'll have time together later," he said with another smile before he turned away and stepped back into the crowd.

Nicholas wanted to be the girl's friend, but he knew it wouldn't happen here, and he knew it wouldn't happen while she was immersed in herself. His time would come, he hoped. He would have to be patient.

TWENTY minutes later, Nicholas stood in front of the mall's gaudy Christmas display. It was made up of a thirty-foot-tall fake Christmas tree and a platform on which sat a fake Santa Claus surrounded by high school girls dressed up as Santa's helpers, taking photos. A long chaotic line of kids and hassled parents waited.

Mary Roberts stood in the middle of the line with her

four younger children. The twins giggled in anticipation, and Billy squirmed in her arms. Amanda simply stared sadly at the fake Santa. From her vantage, his dark hair was visible under the wig and beard. She frowned and turned away.

Maybe Jared's right, after all, she thought sadly. *Maybe there really is no Santa Claus, and I should just accept it. I'm a big girl. I can handle it.*

Amanda let her eyes wander around the crowded mall—from the fake tree to the bustling crowds—from the harried looks of moms and dads to the frazzled nerves of the mall workers—from the fake Santa to the real Santa....

Wait!

She stopped suddenly. Her head jerked back to the spot where she thought she'd seen him. It was only a peek, but she knew it was him. She craned to get a better look, when suddenly the milling crowd seemed to part for her, and there he stood—the plump little man she thought she'd seen seconds before.

To her shock, he actually looked like Santa Claus. He had a real beard and real white hair with a jolly looking face and a sparkle in his eye.

At that exact instant, Nicholas turned and looked directly at Amanda. He waved at her. As quickly as she had given up hope that a real Santa actually existed, her hopes were renewed. A huge smile spread across her face. She lifted her hand slowly and waved back. She stepped out of line and walked toward Nicholas.

"You're him, aren't you? You're the real Santa Claus," she said as she stood in front of him.

"Yes, I am," Nicholas beamed at her. Although other children noticed Nicholas, no one else stopped to acknowledge him—so, at least for a brief time, Amanda had him to herself.

"I knew it. I knew it as soon as I saw you." Amanda reached for him and hugged him hard for a long moment. Nicholas hugged her and patted her back gently.

"And you, my dear, are..." he started as he reached into his memory bank. "Oh, yes...Amanda Roberts. What can I bring you for Christmas?"

Amanda hesitated for a moment before nodding and answering. "Well, Santa...my mom says we should all hope and pray that our father comes home...and I really do want that. Can you help us?"

"I don't know," Nicholas's smile disappeared for an instant. "Your father has his own mind. It is up to him to make his decisions. No one can force him to come home."

"But that's the only thing my mother wants," she said sadly.

Nicholas stared into Amanda's pleading eyes. Other

children began to take notice of Nicholas and Amanda talking. A ripple of recognition spread through the lower mall and to the Christmas display where the fake Santa was working.

"I promise you that I will do my best, Amanda," Nicholas finally said. "I'll need your help, though. You'll have to keep praying for his return." He smiled again, "But what about you? What do you want?"

"Just that, Santa—if you...." She was suddenly interrupted by a surge of other children crowding toward Nicholas. Slowly, Amanda was pushed away. Nicholas began hugging the children who were swarming around him. Amanda turned to walk away, and Nicholas called out, "Amanda!"

When she turned to him, he mouthed, "You'll get your bike this year."

Amanda clapped her hands sharply as Nicholas waved and said, "Merry Christmas."

"Merry Christmas," Amanda whispered happily.

Nicholas laughed and joked with the excited children and weary mothers as Sarah emerged from yet another store with an exhausted Stevens trailing behind her. She stared in shock at the children surrounding Nicholas. She grew angrier with each moment and each happy hug.

Stevens stood behind Sarah. He placed his packages down on an empty bench to rest his weary arms, when he too suddenly spied Nicholas. Despite his fatigue, his reaction was different than Sarah's. He chuckled at the scene of kids swarming around the little man.

"What's he doing, Mr. Stevens? I want you to get him... now!" Sarah demanded.

Stevens' smile faded. "I'll leave the packages here and get him, Miss Sarah," he said before he trudged toward Nicholas.

ON the mall's second level, just above all the commotion, Jared, M.J., and Hammer walked like town toughs among the milling shoppers. Jared glanced over the rail, and his buddies followed with their own looks.

"Hey, look, Jared...there's your mom," said M.J., pointing.

"Yeah. But who's that old guy?" he asked, nodding to Nicholas.

"Santa Claus," said Hammer sarcastically.

M.J. and Hammer began to laugh while Jared scanned the crowd and then stared again at Nicholas, who suddenly looked directly at him. Their eyes locked. Nicholas smiled broadly and waved an arm at Jared, beckoning him to join the crowd. Jared pulled away from the rail sharply. "Let's get outta here!" he commanded.

Hammer and M.J. looked quizzically at each other but followed Jared.

"Hey, wait; where's Burner?" shouted M.J.

Jared turned. He was still flustered at the little fat guy's seeming recognition of him. He shook his head angrily, both to clear his mind and because they now had to search for Burner. After a few seconds, Jared spied Burner preparing to lift some chocolate from a candy store. Burner looked around furtively to make sure no one would see him. He then suddenly reached for one of the packages of chocolates on display. Almost immediately his hand was pushed away and he turned sharply to face Jared who glared angrily.

"Don't be stupid. Security is staring right at you."

Burner glanced past Jared to a security guard, who was, indeed, looking directly at him.

"You want to blow our whole plan?" Jared whispered. "We got something much bigger going. C'mon."

BACK on the mall's first level, Nicholas had calmed the children and gotten them to sit quietly on the floor in front of him. They were transfixed with broad smiles and bright eyes as Nicholas spoke softly of how busy his elves were at the North Pole and how if they all were patient and good, they would have the best of Christmases. Stevens pushed his way through the throng and was finally able to maneuver next to Nicholas.

"Come, Sir, we must move on," he whispered.

"Just a few minutes, Jonathan," Nicholas responded. "Please stay with me."

Nicholas turned back to the children as Stevens glanced back to an angry Sarah. He shrugged to her and turned back to Nicholas.

"Do you see that man up there?" Nicholas asked as he pointed to the fake Santa.

The children turned quickly, returned their gazes to Nicholas, and nodded. "He and many others are my helpers. What you tell him always gets back to me, so when we're finished here, you must go back to that man and get your pictures taken with him so that you'll all have a memory of this Christmas, okay?"

Then, amidst the nods, he leaned forward conspiratorially, and the children fell silent.

"Now, I want to tell you all a little secret. When I'm here in person, none of you has to tell me what you want. All you have to do is close your eyes...be very quiet and think very hard about the present you want. I'll know."

All the children and some adults did exactly as Nicholas suggested.

"Come, Sir, Miss Sarah is waiting," whispered Stevens again.

Nicholas glanced past him to Sarah, who fumed off to the side. "Just a few more minutes, Jonathan," he pleaded.

Nicholas then turned back to the children, who had begun to open their eyes. He looked at one six-year-old boy.

"Come up here, my boy," he beckoned.

The little boy was not shy. Nicholas threw an arm around him as he ran up and turned him gently to face the still growing throng of children and adults.

"I must leave right away, but before I go, I'd like to do something. Jimmy here would like to lead us in a song—wouldn't you, Jimmy?"

Jimmy nodded vigorously before he turned back to one of his friends with wide, glowing eyes and a broad, open-mouthed, gap-toothed smile.

"And my friend Jonathan will help him." Nicholas put his free arm around Stevens and pulled him closer.

Stevens was shocked. His eyes bulged, and his jaw dropped open. He struggled to pull away from Nicholas, his head shaking "no" just as vigorously as Jimmy's head had bobbed up and down only seconds before.

"Do all of you know 'Silent Night'?" Nicholas asked.

"Yeah!" shouted the children and parents alike.

"All right, so we all remember the birthday we are celebrating this Christmas, let's sing together." Nicholas turned to Stevens, who was still trying to pull away. "Please join us," he whispered.

Jimmy's face grew serious. He started to sing the first words of the Christmas favorite. His voice was scratchy and off-key, but loud enough to get sporadic other voices in the crowd to join him. Nicholas continued to stare pleadingly at Stevens, who relaxed somewhat and began to look at all the happy faces that had gathered around this unusual little man.

Stevens smiled slowly as the crowd struggled to follow Jimmy in singing his favorite carol, the very one his mother had sung so sweetly to him and his brothers when they were children. The crowd completed the first verse, and Stevens turned to Nicholas, nodded, and stepped forward to stand next to Jimmy. The crowd was suddenly silent at the end of the verse, and Stevens started the verse again.

"Silent night," his rich tenor intoned as Jimmy looked up and the crowd stared. "Holy night," he continued while Nicholas began waving his arms frantically for the crowd to join Stevens. "All is calm; all is bright."

Jimmy and the rest of the crowd, now having a lead voice that was strong enough to follow, joined Stevens, this time in loud resonant tones that carried throughout the mall. They sang all the verses with a joy that was suddenly contagious to shop workers, passersby, and everyone within earshot—except for one. Sarah stood stone-faced and angry, unable to walk away for fear of getting lost. When the song finally ended, Nicholas led everyone in a loud ovation.

"That was wonderful," he said. "Now find your parents and have a wonderful Christmas; I'll see you all very soon."

A quiet peace ran suddenly through the crowd. Parents and children alike waved at Nicholas and Stevens, and they whispered, "Merry Christmas." When the crowd finally dwindled away, Nicholas turned to Stevens.

"Well Jonathan, it appears you haven't lost the beautiful voice you had as a child."

Stevens simply smiled, lost for just a few more moments in memories of Christmases past.

"Thank you, my friend," Nicholas continued. "We needed the strength of your voice to get the parents to join the singing."

"Thank you, Sir," Stevens said before suddenly realizing that he had left Sarah alone. "Oh, Sarah.... Where is Miss Sarah?" he asked as he turned and frantically scanned the remnants of the crowd for the girl.

"There," Nicholas pointed and began to make his way to the girl with Stevens following anxiously behind.

SARAH was bright enough to understand her sulking and pouting were getting her nowhere with Nicholas. She knew she was supposed to be the center of attention, but Nicholas didn't seem to understand that. She tried the commanding air again as Nicholas approached. She hoped he would show the same concern for having abandoned her as Stevens was showing, but he didn't.

"Did you enjoy the singing?" he asked, ignoring her look.

"My Daddy hired you to stay with me, not all those others," Sarah said, ignoring Nicholas's buoyant mood and the fact that he hadn't been hired at all. "You were supposed to be with me all day."

"But Mr. Stevens was helping you, Sarah...and doing a very good job. You didn't need me," Nicholas responded.

"Yes, I did. More than those others...I.... You were supposed to be with me!" she declared. She turned away to hide the tears of frustration welling up in her eyes and ran toward the exit.

Nicholas and Stevens glanced sadly at each other and followed the young girl, who suddenly looked so small and fragile.

In the back of the car on the way home, Sarah stared out her window. Nicholas waited for several minutes before speaking quietly. "I was hoping you'd want to join us, Sarah.

This season is not just about gifts. It's a time of joy, of song, and most of all, my dear, it's a time for all to share with others and try to bring happiness to those who are less fortunate than we are."

"No!" Sarah turned sharply and shouted. "No...I don't want to hear anymore. I share enough. I share my daddy with the whole world. I don't have to share anything else."

She again turned away and glared angrily out, into the passing world.

~ 5 ~

By the time Jared returned home, day had settled into early evening. He turned up the potholed driveway, hands stuffed in his pockets and his head bowed, deep in thought over the day's events. Suddenly, out of the shadows, a tall, burly figure leaped at him and grabbed his arm. Jared jumped away and struggled desperately against the attacker, who was a good six inches taller and at least one hundred pounds heavier. The youth kicked and struggled to free himself from the man's grasp before he was suddenly shoved backward.

"Hey, relax," the man shouted. "I got news for you."

Jared recognized Enrique (Hank) Hernandez, Hammer's uncle. He worked on the grounds at the Stone estate. At thirty years old, Hank was strong, muscular, and still a local gang member of considerable repute.

"God, Hank...you scared me to death," Jared whispered angrily.

"I'll do more than that if you screw this up, punk." Hank stepped fully into the light and glared at Jared, who returned a defiant glare of his own. Hank continued with a chuckle, "You think you're tough, huh? We'll see if you can pull this job off."

"What do you want?" Jared asked.

"My girl's leaving the library window open tomorrow night. You know where it is?"

"Yeah, if your layout of the house is right."

"It's right, man. Let's see if you and that good-for-nothing nephew of mine can do something right."

"Don't worry," Jared shook his head and turned slowly to the house, listening carefully for any sudden move from Hank.

"Don't mess with me, man," Hank warned as he turned with a self-satisfied grin and nonchalantly walked away.

NICHOLAS unpacked toiletries and clothing, stopping occasionally in surprise at some of the modern items he was pulling from his case. When he was nearly finished, he reached in for the last item, a small glass globe perched atop a wooden base. Inside the globe was an intricately carved scene of a stable in which Joseph and Mary knelt, looking adoringly over the baby Jesus in a manger. The three figures were surrounded by figurines of shepherds kneeling before Jesus'

"Wrong?... No, Miss. Nothing is wrong." His half-smile broadened slightly, and Miss Grundick's usual frown turned down even more.

"Well...where are you going with that ridiculous grin?"

"Oh...just to make sure all's well upstairs...with Miss Sarah...."

"Yes...well, make sure our guest is gone early in the morning—before she wakes."

"Yes, Miss...I will."

Miss Grundick stared hard at Stevens for another minute, finally shook her head, and turned back into the study. Slowly, from between Stevens' feet, Nicholas pushed himself up off the steps where he had been lying on his stomach in the shadows.

"Are you all right?" asked Stevens.

"I really am too old for this, you know." Nicholas smiled and motioned Stevens onward.

SARAH lay on her bed, her right arm clutching a large stuffed bear under her chin. She was watching the movie, *Miracle on 34ᵗʰ Street*, when suddenly she heard a soft knock at her door. She reached for the remote control, turned off the TV, and scurried under her covers. The door opened slowly and

---

crib. Nicholas smiled and placed the globe on the end table next to his bed. He removed his coat, worked on the bowtie, and sat on the edge of the bed, tired and pensive. He stared at the Nativity scene.

"Dear Lord," he began to pray softly, "please help me with this child. She is so sad and angry...yet I don't know how to reach her. Please show me the way."

At that moment there was a light knock at the door. It opened slowly, and Stevens poked his head into the room.

"Jonathan. Nice of you to drop by." Nicholas perked up, but the sad look on Stevens' face made him drop his head. "I guess Sarah is still pretty upset."

Stevens nodded his head. "Yes, Sir, I'm afraid so." He hesitated for a moment, not wanting to say what was coming. It was surprising to him that he had grown fond of Nicholas in such a short time. Stevens was deeply moved by the events at the mall. It was as if a breeze of pure happiness had suddenly blown into the Stone household, and despite his initial misgivings and his charge from Miss Grundick to have Nicholas out of the house, he knew that, given enough time, Nicholas could break through the angry shell Sarah erected around herself after her mother's death. Yet he had entered Nicholas's room for a reason, and with a sincere heaviness of heart he had to break the bad news to his new friend.

"I'm so sorry to say this, but Miss Grundick has instructed

me to tell you that you are to leave first thing in the morning."

"Does Mr. Stone know this?" asked Nicholas.

"Yes, Sir...I believe so. Mr. Stone just came in. Miss Grundick told him how upset Miss Sarah was. I believe Mr. Stone made the decision."

Nicholas nodded slowly. "I understand," he said.

"I tried to speak up for you. You were quite impressive today at the mall. You were wonderful with the children."

"That was fun, wasn't it?" Nicholas said wistfully.

Stevens smiled sadly. "I'll take you where you wish to go in the morning."

"Yes, I'll be ready."

Stevens stood but hesitated before leaving the room. He was suddenly deep in thought.

"Is there something else, Jonathan?" Nicholas asked.

Stevens suddenly looked at Nicholas.

"I think you should see Sarah," he said conspiratorially. It struck him how very important it was for Nicholas to talk to Sarah before he left. He couldn't explain his thoughts clearly, but he knew Nicholas could help the girl. He was sure the little man could bring some happiness into her life.

Nicholas brightened as Stevens glanced back at the door and then whispered, "Wait one minute."

He opened the door, glanced down the hall, and turned back to Nicholas, putting a finger to his lips and waving for

him to follow. Nicholas grabbed the Nativity glo[...] lowed Stevens out of the room on tiptoes. They r[...] tiously down the hall, past the study, where Miss[...] sat reading, and to the stairs. Only a few lights bur[...] hall, but they were sufficient to cast long dark shado[...] wall opposite Miss Grundick, and the ever-vigilan[...] looked up suddenly.

"Stevens...is that you?" she asked.

Stevens blanched and stopped short in his tracks[...] las, a step behind him, continued his pace and bump[...] Stevens. Both men hushed each other and tried des[...] to untangle themselves from each other. It took sev[...] cruciatingly long seconds for Stevens to compose h[...] and answer.

"Ah...yes, Miss."

"Have you told him?"

"Yes, Miss."

Miss Grundick frowned at the stilted responses and[...] waited for more from Stevens. When nothing further wa[...] fered, she stood and marched to the study's entry. She c[...] see Stevens in shadow, standing on the third step and se[...] ingly staring directly at her. As her eyes adjusted slowly to[...] hall's dim light, she could discern Stevens' half-smile, whi[...] looked as if he knew he'd been caught doing something.

"Is anything wrong, Mr. Stevens?" she asked.

Nicholas's round, white-maned head pushed through the opening.

"May I come in?" he whispered.

Sarah breathed a sigh of relief that it wasn't Miss Grundick. She wasn't quite sure how to react to Nicholas, however.

"I came to apologize to you, Sarah," Nicholas started.

The effect of that statement was immediate on Sarah. She now knew she had the upper hand, even though she had no clue what she had the upper hand in. She sat up and looked imperiously at Nicholas, who ignored the look, to her dismay. He reached for a desk chair and pulled it up to the bed.

"I'm sorry for what happened this afternoon, Sarah. I'm not quite sure how to say this," he began again.

Sarah leaned forward, surprised that an adult would confide his weaknesses to her.

"I have this terrible need inside me to help other people," Nicholas continued. "Particularly at Christmas time. I just want to help people enjoy and appreciate this happy time. When I saw all those tired, busy people running around the mall and no one was smiling, I realized there was little joy there. I wanted to brighten things up a little, and you and Mr. Stevens seemed quite happy with what you were doing. I guess I was wrong."

He eyed her in hopes she would soften with his apology and explanation. But she didn't.

"Yes...you were wrong," Sarah scolded. "I needed you to help me." Sarah folded her arms in front of her, nodded, and stared at Nicholas.

He stared at her sadly. Finally, he shrugged resignedly. He put his hands on his knees and began to stand. "Well, I'll leave you to your movie. It's a very good one. You really should watch the end of it. Good night, my dear."

Sarah was taken aback. She'd turned the TV off before he'd entered. How was it possible he knew it was on, much less what movie she was watching?

"Wait! What do you mean? I'm not watching any movie."

"No, that's true, but you were before I came in. You were watching *Miracle on 34th Street*, one of my favorites."

Sarah's mouth opened slowly. How could he have known? There had to be an explanation for all the magic she'd witnessed surrounding this round man with the constantly smiling face, but all she could do was stare and come up with one simple question.

"You're not *really* Santa Claus, are you?"

"Why yes, my dear." Nicholas turned and responded quickly. He started to walk hesitantly back to the vacated chair. When she appeared interested, he sat again. "I am the real one. Why is that so hard for you to believe?"

"Well...Miss Grundick and my father told me there wasn't a Santa Claus. It was just a story...that's all."

"Don't I look like the real Santa Claus?"

"Yes...but there are probably a lot of men who do."

"What does Mr. Stevens say?"

"Stevens?" Sarah hesitated and thought for a moment. "Well, I've never asked *him*. But my father and Miss Grundick wouldn't lie to me."

"Oh no, Sarah. I'm not suggesting they're lying. They have simply forgotten. Unfortunately, a lot of adults forget. They start thinking the thing forgotten doesn't exist. Then they teach their children to forget, and it starts a terrible cycle of lost hope."

Nicholas realized he actually had the young girl's attention for the first time. He prayed that he could keep it as he settled in and began to tell her a story.

"Many years ago, your father believed very strongly in me. When he was a little boy, he was so happy and loving. He didn't just believe; he *knew* I existed. The same is true of Miss Grundick. She was a beautiful, smiling little girl. Both of them knew what Christmas was all about and that I was there to help all children understand the wonder of the birthday we celebrate on Christmas day.

"The problem is that so much time passes between each Christmas that your father, Miss Grundick, and many other grownups simply forget. They get caught up in their own worlds of work, pressure, and money. Soon, memories of that first Christmas and what Jesus' birth means to all of us begin to fade. Christmas for them is just a chore that they must fight through every year. For some people it's nothing more than a very big expense, and for others it's just loneliness because they've forgotten. And do you know the worst thing about that, Sarah?"

She shook her head, waiting expectantly.

"The worst thing is when they make their children forget. You see, when the children forget, it creates a wall I can't break through. The children simply harden their hearts, demand the toys and gifts of the world and forget the real gift of God's love and giving."

Sarah stared hard at Nicholas, wondering at his mention of God. Although a part of her wanted so badly to understand the depth and truth of Nicholas's words, all she could grasp was that her father had lost something...much like Sarah had.

"Why did God let my father forget?"

"Oh, He didn't let anyone forget," Nicholas rejoined softly. "Everyone has his own free will. That was God's gift to all of us. We are able to make our own choices. Unfortunately, so many people make choices that make them unhappy. It really is easy to choose to believe, and if that choice is from the heart, everything is so much better."

They stared at each other for several seconds before Sarah dropped her head in thought.

"You see, Sarah, that's part of my problem," Nicholas rejoined. "I believe so strongly that I just want to help others believe. Because of that, I upset you today." He hesitated for several seconds, and when he received no response from Sarah, he continued, "Well, it's late. You should get some rest. I'll be leaving in the morning, so I'll say goodbye now."

"Where are you going in the morning?" she asked, surprised. There was something important in Nicholas...something she had to pursue. Why would he be leaving?

"Your father was very concerned that you were so upset today."

"He was?"

"Yes, of course he was. He loves you. He didn't want me to stay if I upset you. I've been asked to leave."

"I don't want you...you said you were sorry. Don't you want to stay?"

"With all my heart, but I must leave in the morning." Before standing, he reached into the pocket of his coat. "I have something for you."

It was the Nativity globe. He smiled and handed it to her. Sparkling stars were cascading down around the manger. Sarah's eyes went wide as she accepted the beautiful gift. She had never seen anything so colorful and beautifully carved in all her life.

"Merry Christmas, Sarah," Nicholas said and turned to leave.

"Merry Christmas," Sarah whispered. The door closed behind Nicholas, and she continued to stare at the wonder of the gift.

When Sarah finally looked up and noticed Nicholas was gone, she sat quietly and held tightly onto the beautiful glass globe.

TWO hours later, Jonas Stone was sleeping soundly in his room when, from the fringes of his dreams, he sensed someone standing over him. His eyelids shot open, and through the haze of sleep, he was finally able to discern his daughter.

"Sarah...what's wrong?"

"Daddy, please don't send him away."

"What?... Who?"

"Nicholas, Daddy. Don't send him away tomorrow."

"Sarah, it's almost midnight."

"I'm sorry, Daddy. I just couldn't sleep. Please don't send him away."

"I thought he upset you."

"No, Daddy...he's...he's fun. Please let him stay...please."

Jonas shook his head slowly. He was sitting up, rubbing his eyes and yawning as his daughter pleaded with him. He was groggy and in no condition to argue with Sarah.

"I'll let him stay another day," he finally said through another yawn. "We'll talk more about it tomorrow."

"Thank you, Daddy," Sarah hugged him.

At first Jonas was taken aback by his daughter's hug—a hug he hadn't experienced in quite some time. Slowly, he raised his own arms and hugged Sarah back.

"Let's get you back to bed." He stood, threw an arm around her, and walked her back to her room.

~ 6 ~

The next morning Nicholas was packing his bag when Stevens walked into his room, beaming.

"He changed his mind."

"What's that?" asked Nicholas.

"Mr. Stone changed his mind. He wants you to stay on."

"And Sarah?" Nicholas asked warily.

"Oh, she's very excited. I believe it was her doing. I overheard something about her waking her father last night after midnight."

"That's wonderful," Nicholas smiled just as Sarah bounced into the room.

"You'll stay?" she asked.

"Yes...and I have the perfect outing. That is if Mr. Stevens here can drive us."

"Miss Grundick would be delighted to have us out of the house today...last minute preparations for the party tonight. I'd be glad to accompany you." Stevens bowed jokingly.

"Can Daddy come?" Sarah asked.

"Of course, if he'd like," answered Nicholas.

Sarah took Nicholas's hand and led the two men into the foyer, where Jonas Stone was giving Miss Grundick instructions for the party that evening. He was dressed in his suit and clutched his black leather briefcase at his side.

"Daddy, can you come with us today?"

Jonas turned at his daughter's interruption. He appeared preoccupied, seeming to have forgotten the previous night's hug. When he finally answered, he smiled, but gave his daughter his usual reply.

"I can't, Sarah. I've got a big meeting today at work. I'll see you at the party tonight, though."

As Jonas was putting on his overcoat, he stared hard at Nicholas. Although his daughter was pouting, he paid no attention. Instead, he motioned to Stevens to join him as he walked out the door and whispered, "Stay with them Stevens...at all times."

"Yes, Sir."

Several minutes later, Nicholas helped Sarah with her coat and tried to think of something to say to console the girl. Miss Grundick took Stevens aside and instructed him on his duties for the day.

"I don't want to hear that he's a harmless little man, Mr. Stevens. I don't trust him. I don't understand why Mr. Stone changed his mind, nor do I understand why you now defend him. Make no mistake; he is not to be trusted. Watch him closely," Miss Grundick commanded icily.

"He speaks well of you, Miss," Stevens responded with a smile. "He says you were a very beautiful little girl...full of life and...."

Miss Grundick was suddenly perturbed. "Yes...well... that's behind us now, isn't it? He didn't know me anyway."

"I believe he may have known you, Myra."

"Myra? You forget yourself, Mr. Stevens," she nearly shouted. "Are you losing your wits too?"

"Perhaps I'm just finding them again."

Miss Grundick stared for a moment at the man, not quite sure what to make of him. Stevens, on the other hand, was enjoying the woman's discomfort and smiled broadly.

"Go Mr. Stevens, and be very careful. The man is dangerous. I feel it. Make sure you're back early for the party. Mr. Stone insists on Miss Sarah's presence."

She glared at him. Stevens nodded and followed Nicholas and Sarah out the door. Miss Grundick turned and walked away from the door, past a mirror in the hall. She caught a quick glimpse of herself, stopped, and turned to see her reflection. She primped a little and then, regaining her haughtiness, marched out of the room.

NICHOLAS glanced at Sarah, who stared sadly out the car window.

"I'm sure your father would have..." Nicholas started.

"I don't want to talk about that now." She glanced sadly at Nicholas for a moment before she asked, "Where are we going?"

Nicholas nodded and smiled conspiratorially as he leaned toward her. "If I tell you, it'll spoil the surprise. Let's wait and see."

Sarah smiled and then turned to stare out the window again, when suddenly she saw four boys about her age standing on a street corner, staring at her car. She frowned at the boys and looked more closely at the neighborhood through which Stevens was now driving. Her frown turned to disgust at the dilapidated structures and horrific conditions of the homes, businesses, and the area she knew with horror as "the Sink."

From the street corner, Jared and his friends looked with equal disdain at Sarah's car.

The Mercedes continued through the main streets of the slum; the signs of poverty were everywhere, and Sarah's disgust was heightened. From children clad in what looked to her to be rags the maids in her home wouldn't consider using to wash the floors to barely standing structures that served as homes her father would not even consider for his dog, squalor was everywhere. She was so stunned by the terrible sights she couldn't even speak. Stevens turned the vehicle past two pitted brick columns, which at one time had served as guard gate columns but now served only as ancient sentinels to the battered grounds beyond. Past a tarnished monument sign that read "Penford Children's Home" in chipped and broken lettering, they drove on a pitted brick driveway to the front steps of an ancient edifice blackened and battered from years of neglect.

"What is this?" Sarah pushed back from the car door, hoping to distance herself from the sight outside her window.

"I've been asked to help with a Christmas party for the children here." Nicholas looked at Sarah in hopes of seeing some sense of sympathy.

"I don't want to come here. I thought we were going to do something fun."

"This will be fun, Sarah. There are children here who don't...."

"I don't care," Sarah interrupted. "I don't want to be here. I want to leave."

"I'm sorry, Sarah, we can't leave now," he said firmly. "I promised a man yesterday that I would be their Santa Claus. They're counting on me."

"I thought you understood! I want you to stay with me. Let them get someone else," the girl pleaded.

"They have no one else. I gave my word. Mr. Stevens has already agreed to assist me." Nicholas again looked at Sarah and tried once more to reach her. "Please come with us. We need your help."

"I don't want to," Sarah turned her disappointment to anger. "You lied to me. I want to go home."

"I'm sorry, Sarah, I have an obligation here." Nicholas opened the door and stepped out of the car before turning back to the girl.

"You can wait in the car if you'd like. We'll be back when we're finished. If you need anything, just come inside."

Nicholas and Stevens walked away from the vehicle with Sarah's muffled shout of "No!" following them up the dilapidated wood steps to the chipped and battered front door.

"Maybe I should stay with her?" whispered Stevens.

Nicholas shook his head slowly, realizing he was still a long way from reaching Sarah's heart. He believed he'd made some progress the previous evening, particularly after she'd bounced into his room this morning, excited at the prospect of his staying on. What he hadn't fully realized until this moment was the impact Sarah's father's rejection had on her. She had reverted fully to the disconsolate, haughty child he had first met. Her defenses were back up, and any chance of finding the loving, compassionate girl inside was on the verge of being lost completely. Nicholas's choice now was critical.

Should he back off from his promise to the home's head administrator and work at lifting young Sarah's spirits, or should he take a hard line and hope it would force Sarah to make her own choice? Her decision could ultimately lead her further into a shell or out into the light of love and compassion. To compound matters, Nicholas's time was short, and he had an even greater task ahead of him. His choice was critical, and it was now.

"No...I believe this is best. She knows where we'll be," he said.

SARAH kicked at the front seat, slammed her hands on her own seat, and began to cry and pout as if someone might see her discomfort and come to her aid. When she looked up with tears staining her cheeks, she realized that Nicholas and Stevens were already in the house and that they weren't coming back. She sobbed for several seconds and then stiffened. She wiped the tears away.

"I'll show them!" she mumbled angrily.

She grabbed her umbrella before sliding from the car. She glanced at the house, at the sound of wild cheering emanating from within. She then turned and looked across the weed-splotched dirt front grounds and finally down the potholed driveway. Although her emotions surged from anger to fear to strength and uncertainty, she again looked to the house and then turned and strode down the driveway. Midway to the brick sentinels and the sidewalk beyond, she realized her hand was in the pocket clutching the Nativity globe Nicholas had given her the night before. As a final act of defiance, she withdrew the beautiful gift and dropped it in the dirt by the driveway. With a new determination, she walked past the sentinels, turned left on the broken sidewalk, and marched away.

Within seconds, Sarah began to change her mind. With every step, the gray, decaying suffering of the poor of the Sink became more apparent to her. The bright, freshly painted colors of Penford Heights' homes and the rich smell of moist soil and grass after a cleansing rain were nowhere in evidence. To compound matters, as she tried to avoid tripping over the uneven surfaces, she glanced up to see four hooded figures approaching her. She slowed her pace; her eyes darted furtively in search of an escape route. When one of the figures stepped ahead of the other three and turned toward her, Sarah stopped.

"Hey, rich girl," the figure shouted and strutted up to her. "What're you doing in the badlands?"

Sarah immediately recognized the boy as one of the young toughs she'd seen out of the car window a short time before.

Burner stepped out in front of Jared and M.J. to join Hammer in mocking Sarah.

"Leave me alone," Sarah whispered.

"Whatsa' matter, rich girl? Too good for us?" Burner rejoined before pushing her on the shoulder and laughing at her growing fear.

"Back off, guys," ordered Jared. He glared at Hammer and Burner before he turned to Sarah. "What're you doin' here?"

Sarah stared back at him, trying to act indignant but clearly unsure of herself in the face of such overwhelming odds.

"Don't give me your high-and-mighty look," Jared said. "You're on my turf now, and your money don't mean nothin' on these streets, girl. Your fancy clothes won't get you nothin' down here...except maybe dead."

Sarah backed away, trying hard not to fall into complete panic. The other boys moved closer and surrounded her with leering smiles.

"Go home to your daddy's money before you get hurt," Jared spoke again. "Or don't he want you?"

The boys again laughed and jeered at her. She dropped her head slowly. Jared recognized her discomfort and realized he had struck a chord.

"Maybe he don't care, huh?" Jared chuckled. "Well, neither do we."

Sarah stood transfixed, head down submissively. Her mind worked feverishly between panic and fear, until she realized there was nothing she could do. She was trapped. She looked up, straight into Jared's eyes as if daring him to act. He smiled, motioned his friends to let her go, and said, "Beat it, girl, before you run into someone who takes a liking to you."

Sarah didn't hesitate once an opening appeared between the boys. She ran through it and barely heard the catcalls and jeers behind her.

"We coulda really gotten her, Jared. Why'd you let her go?" asked Burner.

"That's Jonas Stone's kid. We don't need the cops down here now," Jared said. He shook his head at his friend's stupidity. "You gotta think. All of you gotta think. Let's go."

As the others walked away, Jared stood perplexed, staring after the running girl who had just turned up the driveway to the children's home.

- 7 -

Sarah didn't stop running until she was well within the grounds. She was so terrified of her brush with certain death that she could not even appreciate her escape. She ran until she reached the midway point of the driveway before she finally stopped. Breathing heavily, she turned to make sure no one was following. She then broke down and cried. After a few minutes of trying to compose herself, she spied the Nativity globe lying in the mud next to the driveway. She reached for it slowly, picked it up, and gently cleaned it off. Then, after a moment of indecision, she hugged it close.

INSIDE the great room of the Penford Children's Home, Nicholas had changed into a traditional Santa Claus outfit and looked every bit the part. He was surrounded by nearly one hundred children, some of whom were sick, others crippled, and all of whom were hungry for the attention and love of Santa.

Stevens stood next to Nicholas, smiling broadly at the expectation he sensed from the children. He held a large cloth sack, which looked very much like it had nothing inside. He wore an elf cap and tunic awkwardly on his gaunt frame. Nicholas placed his hands on his knees and addressed the children.

"Have you all been very good this year?"

"Yeah!" they shouted.

Nicholas's smile faded suddenly and was replaced by a cockeyed, quizzical look.

"Well, I guess some of you haven't been so good, have you?"

Several young, rebellious looking boys and girls put their heads down as if to hide because they'd been discovered.

"You know, I was young like all of you once," Nicholas continued. "I always found it hard to be good all the time. You know what I mean?"

The rebels perked up and nodded slowly, hopefully.

"I learned a secret about being good, though. Do you want to hear it?"

All heads bobbed in anticipation.

"I learned it's really not possible to be perfectly good all the time. It's hard work." Nicholas watched the knowing nods from his audience. "What's really important is trying your best to be good. If you try your best, then you'll be good most of the time. And those times you're not so good, if you really are sorry…deep down inside… then you really are trying, and that's what matters."

All the children smiled. None had ever heard that there was an alternative to "being good." They figured if they weren't good, they had no hope of a happy Christmas visit. How great it was to now know about the "trying" thing.

"Now, have you all tried real hard to be good this year?" Nicholas asked.

"Yeah!" they all shouted happily.

Nicholas smiled and looked to a beaming Stevens, who handed him the nearly empty sack. Nicholas reached inside and looked down. When he saw nothing in the tangled interior folds, he reached down farther until he found the bottom and saw a large frozen turkey. He glanced up at Stevens, who frowned and shrugged. Nicholas scratched the back of his neck, deep in thought, and then looked at the children, who stared at him expectantly.

"Before we see what Santa has in his sack," Nicholas started, "why don't we have Jonathan lead us in a Christmas song? How about 'Jingle Bells'?"

The children shouted their approval, and Nicholas leaned toward a perplexed Stevens. "Please lead them. I've got to think of something."

Stevens nodded and took control. This enabled Nicholas to walk over to Mr. David Johnson, the head administrator who had approached Nicholas at the mall the previous day. He took his elbow and walked him into the foyer, out of earshot of the children.

"What's going on, Mr. Johnson?" Nicholas asked. "Why are there no gifts?"

Nicholas hadn't noticed that Sarah was hiding in the shadows to the side of the foyer. She had slipped in just a few moments earlier and was trying hard to compose herself in the hopes that no one would see the fear in her face. Upon Nicholas's approach to Mr. Johnson, she pressed deeper into the shadows and listened intently.

"We didn't get enough donations this year," said Johnson sadly. "There weren't enough gifts for even half the children.... We decided to show the children a real whole turkey." He hesitated a second and shrugged, "The turkey is a true treat for them."

"But that won't feed all of them," Nicholas said.

"We know that, of course. We have three others." Johnson was flustered. "Each child will get a little. What choice do we have?"

Nicholas stared for a moment. He knew Mr. Johnson was trying to do his best with the meager finances available to him. He also knew these children—although they didn't need gifts—did need hope and a belief that the world into which they'd eventually be thrown was a good world, worthy of their youthful love and trust. He glanced heavenward, hesitated for several seconds, and then turned back to his chair. Sarah stepped closer and joined several nurses and orderlies, who were curious about what Nicholas would do.

"Lord, help me," Nicholas whispered as he resumed his seat and the final words of "Jingle Bells" were sung. He stared at the children for several seconds before suddenly smiling and reaching inside the bag. He pulled out a large frozen turkey.

"Mr. Johnson first wanted me to tell you that you're all going to have the biggest turkey feast you've ever had. Here's one turkey." Although the children cheered, the adults looked quizzically at each other, and Mr. Johnson grew suddenly angry. Why, he wondered, would this man make such a statement when he knew there wasn't enough?

Nicholas, meanwhile, reached into the sack and pulled out another turkey, and more cheers erupted from the children. Mr. Johnson was shocked.

"And two more."

Nicholas then enlisted Stevens' aid to hand turkey after turkey to orderlies who stood, nearby, stunned. Even while Stevens was helping, he stared into the sack and saw nothing—yet every time Nicholas reached in, he pulled out another turkey. Finally, Nicholas sat back, exhausted from all the bending, and happily shouted, "And many more in the kitchen just waiting to be cooked."

The cheers were deafening, and the shock that had at first been only on Mr. Johnson's face spread to Sarah. She stared in amazement at the empty sack, which held so much wonder.

"Now, do we have anything else in this sack?" Nicholas asked as he picked it up, scrunched it in his hands to show there was nothing, and then set it down with a bright smile on his face. The children grew silent, and Nicholas again pulled open the top to look inside.

"Looks like there's something in there," he finally said. Stevens stepped forward to hold the sack's top open. Nicholas bent, reached deep inside, and pulled out a box, wrapped brightly with colored paper and ribbon. "Let's see here." Nicholas smiled and repositioned his glasses firmly at the bridge of his nose. He read the nametag: "Kimberly. Where is Kimberly?"

A little six-year-old girl with straight blond hair raised her hand high and stood up quickly. A wide grin spread across her freckled face and exposed two missing front teeth. Nicholas waved her forward with a broad smile of his own. The little girl limped as quickly as her condition would permit to his waiting hug and the box of joy. Sarah moved farther into the room for a better look.

From the moment she'd first seen this jolly little man through the rivulets of water running down her bedroom window, she knew there was something different about him. She believed, of course, that the rain had caused her eyesight to play tricks on her and that the umbrella could not have simply materialized above his head. Even when the squeaky tennis shoes he'd worn onto the marble floor seemed suddenly to change before her eyes, she didn't really understand the significance of the event. All she knew then was the man was different.

As Nicholas now reached into the seemingly empty sack and again and again pulled out beautifully wrapped gifts to distribute to the scores of smiling children, Sarah slowly made her way around the room, all the while staring in wonder at the miracle she now clearly recognized.

After their initial meeting, Sarah had been interested in learning more about Nicholas. But, once he'd asserted he was Santa Claus, her hope that he might be something special in her life was dashed. She realized he was probably nothing more than a harmless little man, and she reverted back to the personality she always used at times of disappointment. She tried to show she was strong and that the disappointment didn't matter. She would simply go about making her demands and controlling every situation, and if others didn't like it, that was their problem.

But Nicholas wasn't like anyone else. When he'd come to her the previous evening, things changed. Instead of walking away in a huff, he'd come to say goodbye and let her know he actually cared. And then he'd given her the beautiful globe, which she now clutched tightly in her coat pocket. He'd given her a gift, not to quiet her or to get back in her good graces. He hadn't done it to get her to like him or to get his job back. She realized he'd done it because he liked her. He seemed to really care for her and not about what anyone else thought. And now he was doing the same for the children of the Penford Children's Home.

Sarah smiled. Her wonder at the magic...no...miracles unfolding before her gave way to admiration for the special man who transformed a room of orphaned, sick, and crippled children, without any hope of any future beyond the miseries of the decaying town outside these walls, into one of pure joy and happiness. And he was doing it for the joy that comes only from giving...a joy she had never felt.

Wrapping paper flew as dolls, trucks, balls, electronics, and assorted other gifts perfectly suited to each child were exposed and Sarah finally began to understand. How selfish she'd been to throw the tantrum in the car, to try to run away, to almost miss the wondrous sight before her. How silly she was not to recognize from the very beginning that this special little man had come to spend time with her…not because he was paid to do it, but because he liked her…he loved her, just as he loved all these children. And when she looked around the room and saw the joy in the faces of Mr. Johnson and every adult, even Mr. Stevens, she realized it was because he loved everyone.

When Sarah stopped walking near the back of the room opposite Stevens and Nicholas, she again surveyed the chaos and smiled. Nicholas stood slowly, stretched his back, and shouted above the din.

"Well, my dear friends, is that everyone?"

All heads nodded vigorously with smiles as bright as stars. Sarah continued to scan the crowd until her eyes fell upon a portable bed just a few feet from her. The orderlies who had wheeled the bed into the room and stood beside it for much of the gift giving had joined the other children in front of the bed and left the twisted body of a young boy lying unattended. Sarah stepped toward the bed in search of the child's gift.

The boy was about six or seven years old, although Sarah couldn't be sure of his age. His body was so small and tightly wrapped with arms and legs entangled at his chest and stomach that she could not really tell. The boy lay on his side, unable to move. From the corner of his lips a thin stream of spittle leaked onto the bed, and nowhere near the child or his bed could she see a gift.

Sarah's heart quickened at the thought that she might help this forlorn child if only she could raise her voice loud enough for Nicholas to hear her. She flushed a bit and then braced to shout.

"No, that's not everyone. This boy didn't get anything."

As loud as the room had been just seconds before, such a silence now prevailed. Everyone turned to stare at Sarah and the little boy on the bed before her. Sarah's first reaction was shock that her words had such an effect. Her stomach jumped for a second as all eyes bored into her, but she stood firm and stared at Nicholas.

A young boy some ten feet from Sarah stood and glanced at the bed. He turned sharply to Santa and said, "Yeah...Greggy didn't get nothin'!"

Nicholas craned his neck and asked, "Gregory didn't receive a gift?" He then looked around himself and then at the flat cloth sack lying at his feet. He lifted the sack and held it up as he walked slowly through the children and their gifts to stand at Gregory's bedside across from Sarah.

"I can't seem to find anything in here for Gregory. It's empty."

Sarah glanced at the young child on the bed and noticed that he was trying to lift the corner of his mouth in a smile at Nicholas who had crouched next to the bed to be at eye level. For several seconds no one spoke. Nicholas smiled sadly and stroked the young boy's head. Sarah's stomach churned at the thought of the one child who needed the most getting nothing. Then suddenly she knew what to do. It was as if she'd been struck with an understanding that had been there all along but only now came forth as the shackles of her self-pity were lifted.

"Wait," she said. "Don't you remember Santa? Your sack was too full."

Nicholas looked up at Sarah, who withdrew the Nativity globe from her pocket and extended it toward Gregory. "You asked me to hold this one for you. It was special because it was for a special boy named Gregory."

Because the boy couldn't turn, Sarah reached over him, laid the globe before him, and flipped the switch that produced the beautiful sounds of "Away in a Manger."

Children erupted in cheers, and the adults tried to staunch the tears that wouldn't seem to stop. Gregory smiled as broadly as his condition would permit, and his eyes gleamed in wonder at the beautiful gift.

ile broadened, and he nodded slowly,

o the window contentedly. She wasn't sure
peace because nothing had changed with
ething had happened to her. She could
mmersed in herself. Her thoughts were of
they experienced through the love of this
nd her own unselfish act.

hing and almost dark as Stevens drove on
Sink on his way to Penford Heights.

left at the next corner, will you? I have
ust do," instructed Nicholas.

s in less than two hours, Sir."

ase."

cholas instructed Stevens to stop in front
holas stepped out of the car and walked
oys in the garage. Jared and his friends
as and then at the vehicle where Sarah's
nouthed and wide-eyed at the window.

k to you?" asked Nicholas.

d. He'd never met this man, and there
r the girl could possibly know his name.
he girl had ratted them out somehow.
ds, who stared back dumbfounded. He
y put and walked to Nicholas.

Nicholas stood slowly and smiled at Sarah. She returned a smile that revealed the joy she felt from giving and her own realization that Nicholas really was Santa Claus. Nicholas took Sarah's hand and squeezed it in thanks. He then laid his other hand on Gregory's head.

"Lord, help this little one with his infirmity," he prayed silently.

- 8 -

Dreary daylight drifted toward dusk before Nicholas and Stevens shook hands with Mr. Johnson and his staff to bid them Merry Christmas.

"You're a miracle man, Mister...Santa," Mr. Johnson corrected himself.

"It wasn't me at all, Mr. Johnson. I am only His tool," Nicholas answered with a quick glance heavenward. "The real miracles here are being performed by you and your staff."

Just outside the great room where the children were starting to put gifts away in preparation for dinner, Stevens turned to Sarah, "Where is your coat, Miss Sarah?"

A five-year-old girl named Julia walked up behind Sarah with Sarah's beautiful coat hanging over her small frame and dragging on the floor.

"Julia liked it so much, I gave it to her," Sarah answered.

"Julia, now give it back. Sarah will be cold without her coat," said Mr. Johnson.

"What do you want? We didn't do nothing to her." He motioned to the car.

"Please, don't do this thing you're planning," Nicholas said.

Jared stared at him for a moment, until it was clear he hadn't come to do anything about the confrontation with the girl outside the children's home.

"What're you talking about?" Jared finally asked.

"You know, Jared. It'll get you nothing."

"Hey, who are you, old man? Get outta here."

"There's another way," Nicholas continued.

"I told you to leave," Jared commanded and took a threatening step toward Nicholas.

Not intimidated, Nicholas nevertheless raised his hand and said, "I've come only to talk."

"Well, I don't want to talk. Now get outta here."

Nicholas shook his head sadly and then slowly turned away.

Inside the house, Amanda, who stared out the window, shouted to her mother, "It's Jared, Momma. He's talking to a man.... Hey, it's Santa."

Mary had lifted Billy and followed the twins to the window to see Jared staring after Nicholas, who walked back to the car. She recognized Nicholas immediately as the man who had so enthralled the children at the mall just the day before. She walked to the front door and called out to her son as the car drove off.

"Jared, what was that all about?" she asked.

"Nothing, Mom. He was just asking directions," Jared responded.

Mary didn't believe him but knew she would not get to the truth in front of his friends.

"It's time to eat," she said to get him away from his friends. "You boys can talk later."

"I'll be right there."

Mary frowned and turned from the door.

Jared rejoined his friends, and M.J. asked, "Wasn't that the Santa from the mall?"

"He knows something," Jared whispered pensively. He tried to understand how Nicholas could know anything. He'd never met the man. And even if Hank's girlfriend had told the man what was going down, he couldn't have linked it to Jared because she didn't know him.

Burner sidled up to his friend and whispered nervously, "What do you mean?"

"I don't know. But he knows something," said Jared.

"Hey, punks...you ready?" Hammer's uncle Hank walked up the driveway at that instant and glanced up the street at the car's disappearing taillights. "What's with the old guy?"

"He was talking to Jared," Hammer responded.

"What about?"

"Nothing," said Jared. "It's not important."

"The fancy old dude didn't come here for nothing," said Hank threateningly.

"Jared thinks he knows something," Burner said.

"Oh, give me a break," said Hank. "Are you girls chickenin' out? He don't know nothin'...unless one of you talked." He turned to Hammer and grabbed him. "Did you talk, nephew?"

"No!" squealed Hammer. "Oww, that hurts."

"Leave him alone, Hank. He hasn't talked," said Jared.

Hank glared at Hammer for a second and then shoved him away. "So what's this about?"

"I told you...nothing...we're ready. That's all," Jared said, angry at Hank's intrusion. "Look, I gotta go in and eat. I'll see you guys at eight o'clock."

AS she stared out the rear window at the receding figure of Jared Roberts, Sarah cried out in one long, frantic breath, "Those are the boys who attacked me! Call the police! Nicholas, we need to call the police."

When she received no response, she turned and saw sadness on his face for the first time. It struck her that perhaps

Nicholas already knew everything she was so frantic about and that the concern written on his face was for that and something she could not yet understand.

~ 9 ~

The grounds of the Stone mansion were awash with lights and decorations of the season as expectations of a wonderful evening filled the air. Valets parked cars while tuxedoed doormen escorted guests through the mansion to a large, brightly lit room with open French doors, which led into a large tent in the backyard. Christmas music was being played by a dance band on a stage under the tent, and tables were beautifully set for dinner around a large dance floor. As people began to mingle, several of the unattached women searched for Jonas Stone, the most eligible widower in Penford Heights. But he was nowhere to be found.

IN his room Nicholas knelt before a crucifix lying on the end table by his bed. He wore a perfectly fitting black tuxedo, which had appeared in much the same way his umbrella, suit, and shoes had previously appeared...with a little help from his friends. Although he looked dapper with the contrast between the black suit and the snow white hair and beard, the sadness he'd felt upon leaving Jared was evident. His hands were clasped tightly before him, and his head was bowed.

"I'm going to need some help with the boy. Please guide my hand, Lord."

He rose slowly, dusted his knees off, and struggled to regain the strength he knew he would need with both Sarah and Jared. Although Sarah's apparent conversion at the children's home was reason for great happiness, Nicholas knew her mind and soul were still fragile. Her reaction to Jared, although somewhat expected, was still troubling. He had hoped she'd be a little more subdued, perhaps even understanding of the difficult living conditions with which the boy was confronted daily. He feared Sarah's mood might still be changed by her father, and he prayed that Jonas would not let her down this night.

Nicholas turned when he heard a knock at his door. It opened slowly, and Stevens entered.

"The guests are arriving, Sir." The butler stopped short and stared hard at Nicholas, who rose slowly to his feet.

"What is it, Jonathan? Is something wrong?"

"Nothing wrong, Sir." Stevens smiled broadly, shaking his head. "You look...well, the suit looks very good on you."

Nicholas chuckled and glanced down at himself. "I suppose it does. Perhaps we should get Sarah and join the guests."

IN his office Jonas Stone stared angrily at Tom Burns, his balding, middle-aged business broker.

"What is this, Tom?" he asked. "A joke?" He slammed his open palm on his desk, stood up, and shot piercing glances back and forth between the two stiff businessmen sitting in front of him, next to Burns.

One of the businessmen, Mr. Kagumo, leaned forward and spoke in a deep, stilted voice. "It is no joke, Mr. Stone. We received word today from Tokyo that our company cannot proceed with the transaction."

When Tom Burns first brought the trading conglomerate from Tokyo to his office more than nine months earlier, Jonas had been leery of a potential partnership. Mokai, Ltd. was well regarded in international trade but known as a tough negotiator...and, perhaps even worse, was ruthless when the company hierarchy believed a competitor was desperate. Jonas's initial concern had been that Mokai would carry its ruthlessness over to its partnership as well. It was that concern that was suddenly being realized.

As Jonas stared at Kagumo and his associate, the commitments he'd already made in anticipation of the signing raced through his head: hundreds of thousands of dollars in lawyer and accounting fees, negotiated and soon to be executed marketing and distribution agreements in the United States and Europe, and commitments of fully a quarter of his company's intellectual and productive capacity to a project that could result in enormous annual profits over a period of the next fifteen years. Yet with one sentence from Mr. Kagumo, it was over. Nine months of day-and-night effort were gone.

"We were supposed to be signing tomorrow, Mr. Kagumo," Jonas seethed but tried to maintain control. "You're telling me the company cannot proceed?"

Mr. Kagumo leaned back uneasily. "Yes, Mr. Stone. We have no choice at this time," he said, less authoritatively.

Jonas realized anger would not change anyone's mind. He turned and walked away from his desk to calm himself. Even though he had to control his anger, they needed to understand his displeasure and convey it to their bosses at home. Somehow, he had to win this deal back. There was still time, but he had to be firm.

"You tell them this business will proceed whether Mokai is part of it or not." Jonas believed that Mokai's withdrawal was another negotiating tactic. If they believed Jonas could make the deal work without Mokai's involvement, they might come back to the table. The truth from Jonas's perspective was that without Mokai the deal was dead. He had to take the chance that they'd believe he could do it without them. "You tell your home office that."

Before Mr. Kagumo could respond, Jonas spoke quickly with more confidence than he really felt.

"Well, gentlemen, if that is your final word...I thank you for coming here today. It's a shame you're too busy to stay for the party." He then shook their hands perfunctorily and turned to Tom Burns.

"Tom, you can show these gentlemen out."

"Jonas, I'm..." started Tom.

"I'll talk to you later," interrupted Jonas with a look that withered him.

JARED slipped a black-hooded sweatshirt over his head. His mother eyed him warily. Her fear that her son would follow the same path so many young men from the slums had followed to a life of oblivion was being realized before her eyes. She knew Jared loved her, his sisters, and his brother, Billy. But she also knew her son's stubbornness. Once he decided upon a path, he could not be deterred. Although she didn't know what he had planned, she felt it was no good, and she was afraid.

"It's almost seven o'clock. Can't you stay with the family tonight?"

"I'm meeting the guys, Mom," Jared responded sullenly, without looking at his mother.

"Can't you forget the guys for one night? I'd like to spend some time with you and talk. I know it's been tough on you since your father left. But you're still part of us. We need you."

"I'll be home early...I promise."

"I'm worried for you," said Mary. "Those other boys are lost. Don't let them take you down."

"Don't worry about me, Mom. I'll be all right," the boy said before finally looking into his mother's eyes. He wanted to hug her and reassure her, but he couldn't. He was not sure of himself and what he was about to do. All he knew was that it was his only choice...the only thing he could do to help his mother and siblings. Since he was the man in the house now, it truly was his only choice.

"I gotta go. I'll see you later," he said and walked out the door.

Mary rushed to the window, parted a tattered curtain, and stared at her son. She began to cry and pray softly, "Please take care of my boy, Lord."

A SHORT time later, Jared found himself again standing at the abandoned train depot's window frame, staring toward the Stone mansion. His three friends sat silently behind him. None of them was joking now. Although none would admit it, they were all afraid.

He said to the trio, "Ready to do it?"

They nodded slowly. Burner motioned toward Hammer and said softly, "Hammer's got a gun."

Jared turned to Hammer, surprised. "A gun?" he asked. Hammer lifted his shirt to expose the weapon. "What for? We don't need a gun."

"Hank said we might need it. It's his," said Hammer defiantly.

"Let's see it," Jared held out his hand.

Hammer hesitated, knowing he held some power while he had the gun. But his hesitation ended quickly when he saw the look on Jared's face. He handed the gun to him slowly. Jared held the weapon, felt its weight, and then tucked it into his own belt. "I'll hold it," he said.

JONAS stared out over the gathering throng of revelers. He had already greeted several people with firm handshakes and a half-smile before he'd been able to excuse himself and jog up the staircase to his room. After refreshing himself and refocusing his attention, he stepped out and looked over the balustrade to the growing crowd. He knew it was his time now to forget the loss of the deal and join those who accepted his invitation to Penford Heights' annual "Party of the Year."

Jonas descended the steps and greeted the most recent arrivals as he escorted them into the tent. His eyes flitted back and forth until he spied a table at which sat Michael Fallon, Jonas's flamboyant but brilliant attorney from the law firm of Morgan, Fallon, Tomes & Kennedy.

Jonas greeted the firm's young associates and moved around the table to Fallon, who stood up to greet him.

"Good turnout, Jonas," he said with a broad smile.

"Yes, it is," Jonas responded and glanced around. "We need to talk for a minute."

He took Fallon's arm and pulled him to the side, where he whispered, "You can call your people off the Mokai matter, Mike. The deal's dead."

Fallon was surprised. Like Jonas, he had believed it was done except for the final signing.

"'The company just couldn't proceed with the transaction,' Tokyo said." Jonas shook his head disgustedly as he quoted Mr. Kagumo. "Nine months down the toilet," he continued.

"We're going to have to rethink the whole business plan if we can't get them back."

"Do you want to talk now?" the attorney asked.

Jonas again looked around at the smiling faces, dancing people, and food being put out for the buffet. He smiled resignedly. "Not now. It'll hold till tomorrow. I'm having a party, remember?"

AT another table Nicholas handed Sarah a cup of punch. She looked beautiful, like a young woman, yet it was clear she was not quite sure of herself.

"He didn't even notice," she said as she stared at her father talking to Fallon.

"He will," whispered Nicholas. "Be patient."

She smiled as Nicholas winked and escorted her out to the dance floor, where they began a fast waltz.

"You dance beautifully, Sarah."

"I'm in cotillion." Sarah frowned at the admission.

"Martha and I love to dance at home...keeps us young," said Nicholas, and he began to breathe a little heavier.

At the edge of the dance floor, Jonas talked to a group of business associates. One of them, a stocky, ruddy-faced real estate broker named Sam Wyatt, looked out at the dance floor and said, "That little girl of yours is sure growing up, Jonas. She looks great."

"Everyone keeps telling me that, Sam. I haven't seen her tonight."

"She's out on the dance floor...with that guy who looks like Santa Claus in a tux. Who is he?"

Jonas's eyes wandered the floor until he finally caught sight of Nicholas and Sarah.

"Who is he, Jonas?" Sam asked again.

"Oh...just some help we hired," he answered absently and stared at his daughter, realizing suddenly that she was indeed growing up. Thoughts of Annie suddenly came to him as he watched his daughter. She looked so much like her mother, a fact he had often acknowledged when she was younger yet that he had all but forgotten in recent years. It had been so painful to see his wife in Sarah's child eyes...to see her in every expression and every movement that he had subconsciously pulled away. He had tried for a long time and finally succeeded in burying the memory of the wife he'd loved so completely. It was something he had to do if he could ever live again. Yet, as he now stared at Sarah, he realized he'd done more than bury the memory of his wife's loss. He'd pushed his only daughter away. A sadness filled him for an instant as all thoughts of the broken Mokai deal disappeared, and he knew immediately what he had to do if he was going to save the one thing that really mattered in his life.

"Excuse me, will you, Sam?" Jonas said.

Jonas walked onto the dance floor and tapped Nicholas on the shoulder. When Nicholas turned to him, Jonas smiled at his daughter and extended a hand. "May I?"

Nicholas bowed gallantly and released his thrilled dance partner to her father, who whisked her across the floor.

JARED, M.J., Hammer, and Burner were crouched in the thick hedges outside the high, slump-stone wall surrounding the grounds. All four were dressed in dark jeans and sweatshirts with hoods. They peeked furtively through the bushes to the police cruisers that seemed to appear almost every time they were ready to clamor over the wall.

"A lot of cops out tonight," Hammer whispered.

"Yeah...it's like they know something," M.J. responded. "That old guy must have said something," he continued nervously.

"He didn't know anything," Jared responded curtly. He tried to control his own fears by taking a hard line with the others. "There's a party here. The cops are cruisin' to make sure it doesn't get outta control."

"Like *that* could really happen," laughed Burner sarcastically. He and Hammer started giggling softly until Jared glared them to silence.

"Why did that guy come to your place anyway, man? He was with her at the mall," M.J. continued, still not satisfied their plan was not compromised. "He's...like...in the family. He knows."

"If he knew, Hank woulda told us something was up. He's here all day. Look, M.J., if you want to back out, do it now. The same goes for you guys." Jared pointed at Hammer and Burner. "I'm going in." He stared at his three cohorts, angry that he had to keep pushing them when he was doing all he could to keep his own fears under control.

"I'm with you, man," said Hammer.

"Me, too," whispered Burner.

"M.J.?" asked Jared.

"I'm in," M.J. finally said.

"Okay...let's move."

The four ran in crouches through the shadows from the hedges to the wall. They peeked around the entry post and saw chauffeurs and security guards milling lazily around the grounds, when suddenly headlights appeared up the street. As Jared pulled back to the others, the beam of a police car began to sweep the street.

"C'mon...quick!" Jared ordered.

They bolted through the entry to some bushes inside the grounds just before the beam swept their former position. They waited several seconds, breathing heavily, alert for the approach of anyone who might have seen them. Finally, following Jared's lead, they ran through shadows toward the library.

BENEATH the tent, Jonas and Sarah danced. Between songs they laughed and talked. Jonas's early surprise at his young daughter's maturity was being replaced with a sense of pride as well-wishers continuously interrupted them and spoke of how beautiful Sarah was. For her part, Sarah was having the time of her life. She had her father's full attention and could actually see the pride he exhibited when she charmed her father's numerous visitors.

Just off the dance floor, Nicholas smiled broadly at the Stones' joy. It never ceased to amaze him how people could be so happy simply by knowing that someone they loved was truly interested in them.

Nicholas sipped from his punch cup and watched Jonas and Sarah complete another dance, just as two of Jonas's business associates approached them.

Tom Burns led Sam Wyatt by the arm. Burns was still smarting from the shocking revelation that the Mokai deal was dead. His already ruddy, bloated face seemed redder still with eagerness.

"Jonas," Burns started, "can we talk?"

"Have you met my daughter, Sarah?" asked Jonas. "Sarah, this is Mr. Wyatt, and this is Mr. Burns."

Sarah smiled politely and shook hands with both men. While Wyatt's handshake was warm and delivered with a genuine smile of friendship, Burns's was perfunctory as he turned again to Jonas and whispered, "Jonas, this is important. Can we talk for a few minutes?"

Jonas frowned and turned away from Sarah. "Tom," he said, "hold on. Can you see I'm dancing with my daughter?"

"Jonas, Wyatt can save the deal. We've been discussing Mokai's withdrawal. Sam can bring them back. We need to talk," Burns said excitedly.

Jonas hesitated and looked at both men. He then turned to his daughter. "Sarah, I'm going to talk to these gentlemen for a moment. We'll dance again...okay?"

Sarah nodded slowly, sadly. "Okay, Daddy," she said as the three men walked away.

She stood alone for several seconds before she turned in frantic search for a friendly face. She finally spotted Nicholas, looking down at his watch and frowning. He turned sharply and strode purposefully out of the tent.

Sarah pushed her way off the dance floor as tears of self-pity filled her eyes. She followed Nicholas.

~ 10 ~

In the darkened library Sarah's maid, Anna, moved cautiously toward the east window. She unlocked and raised it partially. She then turned and scurried out of the room, closing the door behind her. Anna slowed only slightly as she made her way down the hall toward the party where she was helping the servers. She glanced back several times and in so doing almost crashed into Nicholas. In a panic she covered her face and ran into the kitchen. Nicholas frowned after her and picked up his pace to the library.

THE boys hid in the bushes and made sure no security guards were near before Jared reached up and pushed the window open. One by one, the others followed him over the sill, into the room. They were agile and quick in their movements, making virtually no sound until Hammer slid to the ground and accidentally kicked a small table upon which a lamp rested. It toppled to the rug with a thud and then rolled to a stop after hitting the base of the desk. The boys stopped and waited breathlessly for the final thunk of the lamp's contact with the desk and then waited longer, nerves on edge, poised to dive in unison back out the window.

After several seconds, which seemed like an eternity, Jared finally stood. The others warily joined him. They stared hard into the darkness of the room and gradually satisfied themselves that Hammer's clumsiness had not derailed them. Jared led the others to the front of the desk, where he began to fidget with the second drawer, access to which would reveal the riches they all believed awaited them.

As the boys focused on their leader's efforts and M.J. was handing him the crowbar he carried, the room's overhead light suddenly blazed to life. Its intensity was magnified by their heightened senses; they were all blinded and frozen for a second. M.J. dropped the crowbar. The others turned and stood, terrified, as their eyes adjusted. Nicholas was standing at the light switch. Immediately, Burner, Hammer, and M.J. ran and dove out the open window. Jared tripped over the crowbar, jumped back to his feet, and ran to the window, which slammed shut before him. It would not budge as he struggled to open it. In desperation he struck it with his fist, but the window held.

Outside, the other boys picked themselves up and ran.

Jared continued to pound on the window with all his might, to no avail.

"You won't get out that way," Nicholas said.

The boy whirled sharply, a trapped animal looking for any escape. His eyes were wide as he crouched and glanced to each window in the room. They were all shut.

"They're sealed, son," Nicholas continued.

Jared glared at Nicholas until he suddenly remembered the gun at his waist. He fumbled at his belt and withdrew it. He pointed it with shaky hands at Nicholas.

"Let me outta here!" he warned viciously.

"Put the gun down," Nicholas was calm. He stepped toward the boy. "This isn't the way."

"I'll shoot, old man. Let me outta here," the boy warned.

"You don't need this. Please put the gun down."

"You don't know what I need."

"You need hope. This is not the way. Stealing won't help any of you," Nicholas said as he took yet another step toward the boy.

"You don't know anything about me," Jared blurted. His eyes again searched the room for an escape. "This is the only way. Now let me out."

"I know you well, Jared," Nicholas soothed. "Your father has left you. You have taken on his responsibility, my boy.

The world owes you and your family. Perhaps it is the Stones who owe you," he continued as he stepped closer still. "But you forgot the most important thing about this season. It has nothing to do with taking or receiving. It's about giving."

"Yeah," the boy stood straight, "tell that to the rich folks. I got nothing to give."

"Yes, you have, son. You have yourself. You also have a heart with which you can do much good. You just have to stop being angry and find it again. Now, please put the gun down."

"Stay back!" Jared warned again, clearly not interested in hearing more.

Nicholas stopped his advance only three steps away from the boy and held his hand out in front of him requesting the gun. Suddenly, the library door opened and Sarah burst into the room. All chance of a peaceful resolution disappeared. Jared was startled yet again. He swung the gun in Sarah's direction and fired. Nicholas reached for him and shouted, "Jared...No!"

THE band was ending a dance number when the crack of the gunshot thundered through the tent. All heads turned and Jonas immediately ran out with Stevens, Miss Grundick, and others fast on his heels.

Anna, frantic at what she may have been part of, met Jonas in the hall and pointed to the library, eyes wide with shock.

"It will not open," Anna shouted.

"What happened?" demanded Jonas.

"Miss Sarah," Anna stammered as she pointed at the bolted door. "She went in...I heard a gun."

Jonas grabbed the door handle and tried with all his strength to open it, but it wouldn't budge.

"Sarah!" he shouted and pounded on the door. He turned to Stevens. "The key, Stevens!"

Stevens fumbled with the keys before handing them to Jonas.

"I tried the key," Anna cried. "It did not work."

Jonas tried anyway. It didn't work. A crowd gathered around him. Everyone stared at the doors for several seconds until they were suddenly blinded by a bright flash of light that burst through the cracks between, under, and above the doors.

"Sarah!" Jonas shouted again before he directed Stevens and Sam Wyatt to join him. They stepped back and ran together into the door. The door splintered on its hinges but held until Stevens and Wyatt hit it again. This time it crashed open, and Jonas ran in.

No one was in the room.

A gun lay abandoned near the far window, and people scurried about in search of any sign of Sarah. All windows were locked. In the distance sirens blared, and from far back in the crowd of onlookers, a commotion arose.

Jonas turned to the commotion, frantic and shocked to find his daughter gone. A potbellied security guard pushed his way into the room and approached Jonas.

"Mr. Stone," the guard started, "we caught three punks at the side of the house. I think they were trying to break in. They didn't get anything. We called the cops."

"You caught them?" Jonas asked. "Is Sarah...?"

The guard turned before Jonas could finish and directed other guards to drag Hammer, Burner, and M.J. forward. The guards threw the boys to the ground before Jonas, their hands cuffed tightly behind their backs.

"Where's Sarah?" he asked almost trance-like.

"What's that, sir?" asked the potbellied guard.

"Where is my daughter?" Jonas glared at the guard. "My daughter, Sarah, was in here when the gun went off."

"Gun?" asked the perplexed guard. He glanced at the three boys, all of whom were struggling to their feet. "You heard the man," said the guard when he noticed the look of fear at the gun's mention.

The boys stood silently for a moment, until M.J. finally looked up at Jonas.

"We don't know anything about your daughter, Mister... honest."

Jonas stared hard at him. "What happened here?"

All three stood silently glancing at each other from bowed heads.

"Answer him!" shouted the guard and shoved M.J.

Jonas put out a restraining hand and glared at the guard before he spoke again.

"Look, boys, you're already in enough trouble here for trespassing. Don't add kidnapping to it."

"We didn't kidnap nobody," Hammer said.

"My daughter is missing," Jonas responded angrily. "I want to know what happened here...now!"

"Honest, Mister, we didn't see your daughter," said M.J. "When that old guy turned on the light, we ran. Somehow he got Jared. That's all we know."

"Who's Jared?" asked Jonas.

"He's our friend," said Burner.

"He's our leader," said Hammer.

Jonas stared at the boys in silence and deep thought for several seconds. Sam Wyatt and Stevens pushed guests back to the library's entry and out into the foyer. Those who could were craning their necks to catch a glimpse of the boys. Jonas concentrated so intensely on the boys that he seemed to see no one else, and all sound except that from his conversation seemed to disappear.

"You saw an old man?" he asked.

"A little fat man," M.J. offered. "Kinda...kinda looked like...like Santa Claus." He glanced around at his friends and others in the room, clearly afraid that his comment would bring a rebuke of some kind.

"When you ran out," Jonas continued, "Jared and the man were the only ones here?" Then, at M.J.'s nod, he asked, "Did your friend have a gun?"

M.J. and Hammer glanced quickly at each other, afraid to say yes but seemingly understanding that if they lied, things would go much worse for them.

"Yes, sir," M.J. finally responded.

Jonas turned from the boys and walked around the room, deep in thought. A tall, black-mustached, uniformed policeman pushed his way through the crowd and walked up to Jonas.

"What's happened here, Mr. Stone?" the policeman asked.

Three other uniformed policemen approached the security guards and took control of the handcuffed boys.

"My daughter has disappeared," Jonas said, "and that gun was fired." He pointed to the weapon held gingerly by Sam

Wyatt. The policeman frowned that any prints on the weapon may have been compromised.

"Do you have any idea where she may have gone, sir?" the policeman finally asked.

"I think she's been kidnapped...by someone I had working in the house," Jonas responded and stepped back, slumped into a chair, and buried his face in his hands. Wyatt approached the policeman to explain what had happened as he handed the gun to the officer.

Behind Jonas, Miss Grundick stared daggers at an open-mouthed Stevens.

ared looked at her and smiled malevolently. "Yeah, e the rich girl."

You shot at me," Sarah whispered as the realization of ist seconds in the house struck her.

Sorry I missed," he said sarcastically. "I'm outta here," ie turned to walk away.

Stop him!" Sarah shouted needlessly. It was clear he l not walk away.

Enough!" shouted Nicholas. He turned to the boy. "You ot in control here, young man. We are not part of your gang. We don't jump at your every word. You are not a here.' You will come with me and do as I say or you will r be 'outta here.'"

ared was surprised at the power of Nicholas's words.

And you, Miss Stone, will put aside your own selfish s and follow me. You are no better than Mr. Roberts Hopefully, you will both learn to be human beings who t interested only in yourselves."

arah was taken aback by the rebuke. Nicholas started rd the road and the travelers making their way. "Come me," he commanded.

arah and Jared glared at each other for several seconds, ving they had no choice but to stay together and follow olas.

~ 11 ~

The sun rose bloated and orange in the eastern sky…a sky vivid with morning colors and speckled sporadically with cloud puffs splashed with the same hues. The air was biting cold, yet with a hint of the warmth that would come at the sun's full rising.

The hard-packed dirt road was already crowded with dromedaries and donkeys heavily laden with the worldly possessions of travelers who walked next to their beasts or rode in carts pulled behind. Mothers and fathers, weary from their journeys and sore from hard nights in the open, clutched the hands of children and trudged steadily along the road. While most walked and held their robes tight to fend off the morning chill, the rich among them lounged in chaises carried by their retainers. No matter what their station, however, all were traveling to their birth towns to be counted in the world census decreed by the Roman Caesar, Augustus.

It was just off this road, a few miles east of a small town called Bethlehem, that three unusually clad travelers were suddenly and unceremoniously dumped on the ground.

Jared, still dressed in dark jeans, T-shirt, and black sweatshirt leapt to his feet as soon as he hit the ground. He crouched, cat-like, arms at the ready to respond to any attack. His eyes darted in every direction in search of some understanding of his predicament.

Sarah simply stared. Her landing on her posterior was perhaps the softest of the three because of all the layers of her party wear. Despite her usual hatred of dirt and dust, she sat quietly for several seconds, her head turning slowly to take in her surroundings. Her mind raced with the contradiction of her father's library and the arid hillside upon which she sat.

Nicholas, still tuxedo clad, sat for a moment before he smiled, stood slowly, and brushed himself off. He glanced at his two companions to make sure neither of them was hurt, and then he looked heavenward and whispered, "That was a little rough, wasn't it?"

He turned to Sarah and helped her to her feet. "Are you all right, Sarah?"

"Where are we?" she asked.

Nicholas didn't answer. Instead, he turned to Jared, who had jumped out of his cat-like crouch and started to run. The problem was that even though his feet were moving at a high

rate of speed, his arms were pumping, coming faster, he was not moving. He exerting all the energy he could muster was.

"You need not try to run, boy. You Nicholas said.

Jared slowed his pace and finally st at himself, and turned to Nicholas. "Wh we?" he demanded.

"We've taken a little trip. I needed t of you and to show you something. Tim at the Stone house, young man," Nicho growing as stern as his jolly features wou

Jared glanced around suspiciously. and confronted by Nicholas, his one ho self in the open, where he could simply Now that he was in the open, he realize help. Somehow, this little man had con never felt anything like it, and he was wa

"I think I'd rather be back at the chances there," he said while pointing glancing around before dropping his cause he didn't know where he was.

It was at that moment that Sarah "You're the one I saw on the street," she

A short time later the three of them stood at the road's edge and watched a dark bearded man lead a donkey carrying a very pregnant woman. The woman smiled through obvious pain and discomfort, and the man glanced back at her with concern in his eyes. The woman was actually a girl of about seventeen. She was beautiful with dark hair pinned back loosely and bright blue eyes that sparkled with life despite her discomfort. The man, in his late twenties, was her husband. He was tall with a dark complexion and dark eyes and a carriage that bespoke strength of character and commitment.

"We'll be there by nightfall, Mary," said the man. "Can you make it?"

"I'll be fine, Joseph. But please hurry."

"She's about to have a baby," Jared said.

"Is she going to be all right?" asked Sarah.

"She's very close to her time, Sarah. She has traveled a long distance in this condition," said Nicholas.

"Do you know them?" asked Jared.

"Yes," said Nicholas, "and so do both of you."

The boy turned to Nicholas. "I've never seen them before."

Sarah shook her head, acknowledging the same.

"You know them nonetheless," Nicholas said. "It's just that you have chosen to forget."

"Where are we?" Sarah asked again.

"We've taken a little journey...to a place called Bethlehem. We've come to witness the first Christmas," Nicholas said.

Both kids were stunned. Although Sarah, who had witnessed much magic from Nicholas, was inclined to experience more, Jared was having none of it.

"Give me a break, man," he said. "Are you telling me we've gone back in time?"

Nicholas nodded. Jared gawked at him and then at Sarah. He'd never considered hooking up with these two when he and his friends planned the Stone robbery. But he had indeed hooked up with them. For the time being, he had no choice and decided to bide his time, go along with the old guy and the rich girl, and look for his escape.

"Who are you?" he finally asked Nicholas.

"I'm one of the others you've forgotten," Nicholas responded.

"What does that mean?"

Sarah stood to the side. Her mind wrestled with Jared's question and with the knowledge she had of Nicholas. Nicholas glanced at her as the boy awaited his answer. Sarah resolved to reveal the truth...no matter how silly it sounded.

"He's...Santa Claus."

Nicholas smiled at Sarah, took her hand, and turned abruptly to follow the travelers. Jared shrugged, glanced around as if they were both crazy, and trotted after them.

MARY Roberts stood at her kitchen counter, her right hand clutching the telephone receiver to her ear and her left hand covering her mouth. She was trying desperately to hold back the tears that started the moment Amanda had come back from her older brother's room and told her Jared wasn't there and that it looked like he hadn't slept in his bed. A few moments later the phone rang.

"Yes...thank you," Mary said awkwardly and hung up. She turned to Amanda and the twins who were staring at her. Billy sat fidgeting in his highchair.

"What happened to Jared, Momma?" asked Amanda, fear etched in her eyes. "Is he all right?"

"They don't know, honey. The police said..." Mary started as she wiped her eyes and glanced around absently before she resolved to do something.

"C'mon, Amanda," she said. "We have to go see someone."

"Who, Momma?" her daughter asked.

"It's about your brother," she responded. She bustled about to ready the younger kids. "Now help me here, Amanda. We'll see if Flora can watch the kids for a while."

Mary grabbed the twins' hands. Amanda took Billy and followed her out of the kitchen.

DETECTIVE Bruce Phillips hung up the telephone. Several plainclothes police officers sat at monitoring stations set up in Jonas's library. They were awaiting a ransom call and coordinating the field search teams, which had fanned out across Penford Heights in ever-widening circles in search of any possible clue. Jonas hadn't slept and was worn and disheveled in his tuxedo from the night before. He looked thoughtfully at the detective, who shook his head.

"That was the boy's mother," Phillips said. "She was shocked. Apparently, she didn't know her son wasn't at home. I told her to get down to the station and talk to Dexter. Maybe she can help us. Other than that, we've heard nothing yet. We've got the whole force looking for them. Something will turn up."

"Thanks," Jonas mumbled and plopped down heavily in a chair.

"Look...Jonas...why don't you get some sleep?" Phillips suggested. "We'll be here. We'll wake you if anything breaks."

Jonas nodded mechanically. Stevens took his arm, helped him out of the chair, and walked with him out of the room.

~ 12 ~

The sun dropped below the horizon while travelers trudged in loose groups down the hill toward the tiny town of Bethlehem. In the distance the first flickers of the warming fires of shepherds could be seen while in the fading light flocks of sheep huddled together for the evening.

Nicholas, Sarah, and Jared stood at the town's east end, watching Joseph lead the donkey upon which Mary was riding. It was clear to them that Mary was struggling with her burden. Joseph recognized Mary's intense discomfort, and he stopped the animal, helped Mary to the ground, and sat her down against a post in front of the closest inn.

"Wait here, Mary," he said tenderly. "I'll find a place for us for the night."

Mary nodded and smiled through her pain and discomfort, and Joseph walked off toward the door of the inn.

"She's not going to make it," whispered the boy. "I saw my mom like this...just before Billy. She needs help fast."

"Come this way, Jared," said Nicholas, motioning for the boy to accompany him and Sarah.

Jared hesitated for several seconds, not sure whether he should try to help Mary or follow the other two. He turned to Nicholas and Sarah, just as Joseph was walking away from the first inn and approaching a second.

The three watched with concern as Joseph went from inn to inn, only to have doors slammed in his face with shouts of "We're full!" and "Too crowded!" from the proprietors. When Joseph approached the final inn, it appeared as noisy and overwhelmed as the others, but he had to try. His wife was about to give birth and could not do so on the cobbled roads of the town. He knocked. The door opened, and a harried little man looked out.

"Please, sir, my wife is ready to give birth. Could we have a place to stay?" Joseph asked.

The little man was unimpressed with Joseph's plea. He was having enough trouble trying to satisfy the throng of people already inside his inn.

"No room!...Go away!" he said. "We have no more room!"

"I just need a shelter, sir...any shelter," Joseph begged.

"We have nothing!"

Jared stepped forward to address the innkeeper.

"What's wrong with you?" he shouted. "She's pregnant. You gotta help."

The door slammed. Joseph dropped his head to control his rising fear before he turned and walked away. Jared ran to the door, hammered on it, and kicked it. He turned to Nicholas.

"Can't you do anything?"

"Not here, Jared. None of us can. We are only observers. No one can see us. No one can hear us," Nicholas responded.

"What's going to happen to her?" asked Sarah.

Nicholas simply turned to follow Joseph.

Frustrated, Joseph approached Mary, afraid to give her the unhappy news. The young woman sat awkwardly, her eyes closed. Despite her predicament she seemed at peace, with her hands holding her stomach. Joseph touched her shoulder. As she looked up, he shook his head "no." Mary tried to reassure her husband not to give up hope. Joseph crouched next to his wife and took her in his arms while his eyes scanned the streets in search of possible shelter. At that moment a middle-aged woman carrying two large empty water buckets stepped up to Mary and Joseph. Joseph was surprised and stood up between Mary and the woman, who was intently viewing her.

"I wasn't sure if you were making up a story about a pregnant wife back there." The woman pointed to the last inn and then looked at Mary. "It's pretty clear it was not a story. This young woman is at her time."

She gently pushed Joseph aside, bent to Mary, extended a hand, and said, "I know a place... come. It's not much. But it's a shelter. Can you travel?"

Mary nodded slowly and leaned forward to take the lady's hand.

"Come, then," she said, smiling warmly. She turned to Joseph. "Take your wife. I will show you where and come to help when I can."

Joseph assisted Mary onto the donkey, and the woman led them toward a hill and a distant cave.

The three visitors followed for a few steps and then stopped when Nicholas held his hands out to either side to hold his companions back. He appeared to be thinking or listening to some instruction with a confused look on his face.

"Why are we stopping?" asked Sarah.

"Yeah, let's follow them," said Jared.

"We'll see them later. I have something else for you to see now," Nicholas said. His companions watched Mary and Joseph start their trek up the hill.

"What is this?" Jared asked angrily. "We can't just walk away from this."

"Be patient," said Nicholas.

THE three travelers found themselves standing in front of a dilapidated wood structure that looked very much like some of the structures that straddled the streets of the Sink. On either side of the hard-packed dirt road were other squat structures made of clay, stone, and wood. The oil-lit interiors cast their glow in uneven intervals onto the road as travelers either reveled in the public eating establishments or made their way through shops still open in the early evening. The well-heeled people for the most part walked in the middle of the road, holding tightly to money purses and valuables and avoiding the shadows where the homeless and wretched skulked.

In one of those shadows stood a boy, dirty and disheveled, wearing a tattered cloak as his only warmth against the night cold. Although he looked tired and hungry, he stood tall and proud. He eyed the street scene and the parade of visitors to his small hometown. He appeared to be about Sarah's or Jared's age. His name was Simon. Something about the boy caught Jared's attention, and he watched him closely. His bearing was that of a leader, much like the bearing of Jared himself.

In the middle of the road a man in his mid-twenties walked quickly to some destination, with his wife clutching tightly to his arm. The young man and woman were dressed in fine clothing of silk and wool, and it was clear to Simon that these two were strangers to the mean streets, those upon which the wealthy rarely tread. The couple's pace was fast as they hoped to be invisible to the street hawkers and vagabonds who wished to separate them from their money.

As the couple walked past Simon, ten street urchins ran out of the shadows and accosted them. The street urchins were boys aged five to twelve years. They begged, pushed, and grabbed at the man and woman, who tried to break past, all the while looking fearfully at the boys. By the time the couple had extricated themselves from the chaos, they were relieved but failed to notice that the man's money purse had fallen to the ground. Immediately, the boys jumped on the purse, fighting and pulling as the man and woman scurried away.

Simon walked calmly into the melee, started pulling boys out of the pile, and began fighting them for the purse. As fists and feet flew, it quickly became apparent that Simon was the strongest of the bunch, and he finally stood alone, holding the purse aloft. Several other boys rubbed bruised body parts and glared at him. Simon stood ready for more, but no one came after him.

"All right...he got it!" shouted Jared, who knew all along that Simon was special.

"C'mon, Simon," whimpered one of the beaten boys.

Simon opened the purse, pulled out one coin, and held it aloft.

"Come here, James," Simon commanded one of the boys. "This will feed all of us tonight." He handed the coin to the boy. "Take the others with you."

James took the coin and the other nine followed him, massaging their wounds with disgruntled looks. Simon pulled his cloak tighter around his shoulders again and turned up the street in the same direction the wealthy man and woman had gone.

"He's a good man. He must be the leader of that gang," whispered Jared. He watched Simon with some pride.

"Yes, he is," answered Nicholas.

"I like him," Jared said smugly.

"That isn't his money. They stole it," offered Sarah.

"What do you know, little girl?" Jared turned on her sharply. "Those people have plenty; just like you do. If they won't share it, we take it."

"'We'?" asked Nicholas.

"Yeah, ol' Simon there...and me," Jared responded.

"Because you're a leader too? Like him?"

"You got that right," the boy nodded.

"Where's he going now?" asked Sarah.

Simon had walked to the main street and turned the corner to the front of an inn crowded with the wealthier visitors. He stopped and stared toward the hills outside the town. From his vantage he could see an unusually large star suspended high in the sky, casting bright rays directly upon what appeared to be a cave. He was mesmerized for several seconds, when suddenly the wealthy young man and woman whose purse Simon held, stepped frantically out of the inn.

"I was carrying it right here, Elizabeth," the man said, pointing to the belt of his robe. "Those animals...I know they took it." He turned in anger, trying desperately to determine his next move in the hopes of recovering his money.

"Andrew, let's go to the authorities," Elizabeth pleaded.

"For what? What can they do with this rabble?"

By then, Nicholas and his companions had reached the inn, and Jared smiled at the wealthy couple's discomfort. "Yeah, they'll sure be able to do something. They'd never catch Simon," Jared said.

Within another moment, however, it became quite apparent that no one would have to catch Simon. He stepped calmly out of the inn's shadows and up to the couple.

"Hey, what are you doing?" asked Jared.

Simon held the purse up to Andrew. "This is yours. You dropped it."

Andrew was stunned. He reached for the purse, dazed at the thought that part of the "rabble" was actually returning his money.

"Are you crazy?" asked Jared, shocked that this boy would even consider returning the money. He believed that Simon and his gang needed it and deserved it more than these two rich folks. Why would Simon be so foolish?

"They're poor and hungry," Simon said to Andrew. "I took one coin out to feed them all. That will serve as my reward for returning your purse."

Andrew and Elizabeth stared at each other, too stunned to say anything. Simon then looked at the star above the cave and set out toward it. When the young couple finally regained their senses and turned toward Simon, he was gone.

"We must find that boy," said Andrew. "There is hope yet in this world, Elizabeth, and we must do what we can to help someone with that young boy's strength and character." Andrew touched his wife lightly on the arm, and he set out at a trot after Simon.

SIMON made his way up the shallow dirt path toward the cave, over which the unusual star seemed to rest. A stable had been built into the front of the cave with the front half of it protruding outside the cave. The stable entry was crowded with young shepherds while others sat along the path, talking in hushed tones. Although all seemed excited, there was a sense of peace among the shepherds, who spent long days and nights tending their flocks for the meager livings their work provided.

Simon stood, hands on his hips, glancing back and forth between the magnificent star and the shepherds. He puzzled over the appearance of a star so bold and bright yet viewable with the naked eye without pain. He wondered at the seeming joy of the shepherds, who by many accounts were as poor as he.

Although he was orphaned, there was a time in Simon's early years that his father had tried to teach him the Hebrew Scriptures about the coming of a Savior. He hadn't given any of it much thought after his parents died because he had to learn to survive on the streets. Yet some of the lessons had stuck, and he remembered the prophesy. He recalled that a star would lead the way, and somehow he knew that this was indeed that star.

As Simon continued up the slope, he heard one shepherd ask his companion, "Is it the One?"

"It is as the angel said," responded the companion. "He has come."

INSIDE the stable, in a far corner where it joined the cave wall, Nicholas, Jared, and Sarah stood in the shadows.

"They're okay," Jared whispered in relief when he saw Mary reclining comfortably on a bed of warm straw and Joseph on one knee next to her. In Mary's arms was the baby.

Although Mary was exhausted and Joseph was concerned about his wife and child, they both cast warm, welcoming smiles to all who stood at the stable entry.

"There's Simon," whispered Sarah.

The boy pushed his way gently through the shepherds. He stood with the others for several seconds before he stepped toward the new family. He knelt before Mary to get a better look at the baby lying peacefully awake in his mother's arms.

"What's his name?" Simon asked.

"Jesus," Mary replied.

"I have something for him." Simon removed the tattered cloak from his shoulders and handed it to Mary, who laid it gently across the baby. "It will keep him warm."

Mary nodded her thanks and extended a hand to touch Simon softly on the arm. They spoke in hushed tones that the three travelers could not hear. Nicholas and Sarah smiled at the sight of the street tough who showed such tenderness to the baby.

Although Jared too was riveted by the scene playing out before him, he was befuddled by Simon's action. He had watched the boy protect the cloak during the melee in the road for the money purse. He had done all he could to protect his one worldly possession...the item that separated him from the others...the only item that could keep him warm. To Jared, the cloak seemed a garment of high honor to be worn regally, despite its tattered condition, for it was the only one among his band of street urchins. It was his and his alone and woe, in Jared's mind, to the one who would try to take it from him.

Yet Simon had relinquished it without a fight. In fact, he had done it willingly for a baby...a baby with whom, in Jared's mind, Simon had no connection. What bothered Jared even more was his realization that he would not have done the same. How could such a strong leader show compassion, tenderness, and...love...Jared wondered. Leaders were strong, without emotion, ruthless when necessary and, above all, never showed weakness. Yet here was Simon, whom Jared respected, who was different.

The boy's mind was in chaos as he staggered a step closer to the young family. Sarah had taken his hand and tugged to bring them both closer for a better look at the baby.

"Out," came a command from the stable's entry. The woman who had shown Mary and Joseph the shelter bustled through the gawking shepherds with an armful of blankets and a container of bread and cheese for the new parents. "Everyone out," she commanded again. "Can't you see she's just had a baby? Get out...all of you."

The lady then turned to Simon. "You too, boy."

Simon stood slowly, a peaceful smile covering his face. The woman ushered him out of the stable, where the rich man, Andrew, stepped up to him. They smiled at each other and began a conversation that would prove fruitful to Simon and every one of his street comrades.

The Holy Family was suddenly alone except for the three time travelers. Nicholas and Sarah stepped forward out of the shadows. Jared held back, still conflicted...not yet understanding the strange power of this child. Mary turned to them.

"Come forward, Jared," she said. "Join Nicholas and Sarah...please."

Sarah turned to Nicholas, surprised that they were suddenly visible. Nicholas nodded slowly and, with his eyes, motioned Sarah to help Jared. She took his hand again, and together they approached the baby who now lay in a manger.

The boy's mind was a fog. Even though he walked with Sarah, the walk was mechanical. The fact that he now realized he was witnessing something no one from his time had ever seen was boggling him. Of course, he'd heard the stories of Jesus' birth. His mother always tried to talk about it, but it had never taken hold as anything more than a fairy tale. It was something that was fun for little kids to think about at their school Christmas pageants. Nothing more. Never anything more.

Jared, like Sarah, had been stunned upon their unceremonious arrival in the hills outside Bethlehem. How they'd suddenly gotten there was unclear, but what was clear is that they could not have gone back in time. His first instinct had been to fight Nicholas, to resist, to demand release, but when he'd seen Sarah give in to the old man so quickly, he'd decided to wait. There was something different about this tuxedoed old guy who was a caricature of Santa Claus. He decided to go along with the charade and find his moment.

By the time the travelers had seen Mary and Joseph and then followed Simon's exploits, Jared was hooked. He was so immersed in the conditions and circumstances of these people that he completely forgot it was all just some kind of hoax. It wasn't until he stood before the family, trying desperately to understand Simon and the reverence exhibited by him, the shepherds, and Nicholas that the reality of his situation began to overwhelm him.

His mind raced from thoughts of where he really was to why these people of such limited means seemed so happy, so at peace. Simon's actions shocked him. Why would a tough guy who had his own gang give the money back? Give up his only worldly possession? Why would Andrew, "one of the rich people," not try to punish Simon and...why...why would all of them be so moved by the birth of this child?

"We've all been waiting a very long time," said Joseph softly as if in answer to the boy's question.

"What..." Jared stammered. "For what?" he whispered as he again looked at the baby.

"For the peace He brings," said Joseph.

"How...how do we find this peace?" he asked.

"He is your brother, Jared," said Mary. She stepped away from the manger and touched the boy's arm. "He is love, and if you love Him and His people, He will always be with you. He will never leave you."

A flood of regret filled Jared. "He will never leave you," she'd said. How was that possible? Everyone left. His father left. There was no one there for his family...for him...for anyone. Those thoughts mingled with fears of his neighborhood, his need for strength without compassion to contend with it all, and the confusion he felt led him to tears. They were small drops at first, but as Mary reached to hug him, he sobbed.

"Be at peace, my son. Call on Him, and He will be your strength," Mary soothed.

As Jared held onto Mary, understanding seemed to wash over him. This was what life really was...a gentle hug and a love so deep that God would send his only son to teach the world that there was only one true gift...the gift of oneself. Jared realized in flashes of knowledge that he never wanted the money his dad worked so hard to earn. He never really wanted the wealth of Jonas Stone. All he wanted was his dad...the love and nurturing of a father who would give his all to his kids. And in the same moment, he understood what his mother and siblings needed as well. Not Amanda's bike or Billy's blocks, not Katie's doll or Kayla's playhouse...but rather Jared...his strength and his love so they could all feel the peace the boy suddenly felt with the knowledge he was never alone. This child...this son of man...would always be there.

"Remember this day, children. It is His day," Mary said softly and released Jared.

He knelt before the manger next to Sarah and Nicholas.

Sarah stared from Jared to the baby and then to Mary. "I wish I had something to give Him," she finally whispered.

"You do, Sarah..." Joseph spoke. "He asks only that you give yourselves...to Him and to all people."

~ *13* ~

The Stone driveway was crowded with squad cars while the grounds themselves were swarming with investigators. It was into this hive of activity that Mary Roberts and Amanda stumbled. Mary parked her ancient rust-marked mini-van by the curb, and she and Amanda walked up the driveway.

Stevens answered the door to Mary's first knock. He was surprised to see the woman and her daughter as he was expecting more police.

"My name is Mary Roberts." When Stevens showed no recognition, she continued, "I'm the mother of Jared...the boy who disappeared with the young girl."

Stevens nodded slowly and wondered why the boy's mother would come to the house.

"May I speak to Mr. Stone?" asked Mary.

"I'm sorry, Mrs. Roberts, Mr. Stone is not seeing anyone right now," Stevens responded protectively of Jonas.

Mary dropped her head in resignation. Stevens saw a sad, worn woman standing before him. It was obvious she was as devastated by the children's disappearance as Jonas. She looked up anxiously, apologetically, and said, "Yes, I understand...but please, sir, I must speak to him. The police will not give me any news...." She hesitated, dropped her head again, and continued softly, "Only that my son was here to rob the house and now he's disappeared. I just need to hear some news, sir. I know Mr. Stone will have news."

Mary stared at Stevens pleadingly, and Amanda took her hand, held it reassuringly. Stevens' heart suddenly returned, and he began to come to his senses. He opened the door and ushered the two in. "Yes, Mrs. Roberts. I'm sorry. Please come in. I'll see what I can do."

JONAS stood, only slightly refreshed by a morning nap. He talked softly to Detective Phillips. Plainclothes detectives sat around the room, awaiting the ransom call. Everyone was tired and nervous. All drank coffee. Stevens ushered Mary and Amanda into the room.

"This is Mrs. Roberts, sir. The boy's mother," said Stevens to Jonas.

"I'm so sorry, Mr. Stone, for what my son did," Mary stammered as she stepped immediately up to Jonas.

Jonas stepped back, not knowing what to say, and not really understanding how he should react to the mother of the boy who intended to rob him, probably tried to shoot his daughter, and was somehow involved in Sarah's disappearance.

"Is there something I can help you with?" he finally asked gruffly.

"Oh, no; I just came..." Mary started. "Mr. Stone, I need some news about my son. All I know is that he's gone. I can't get any more information."

Jonas stared hard at the troubled mother. He finally looked beyond his own concern and saw the same concern in Mary's eyes. He pointed to a chair.

"Please sit down, Mrs. Roberts." He turned to Stevens. "Stevens...some coffee for Mrs. Roberts? And for..." he pointed to Amanda.

"Amanda," said Mary.

"Some lemonade?" Jonas asked.

"Is Jared in trouble?" Amanda asked and shook her head to the offer of lemonade.

"We haven't heard anything yet," Jonas said. "We're expecting a ransom demand. But...we just don't know."

"Is Jared involved in the kidnapping, Mr. Stone?" asked Mary.

"We...we don't know yet. We just don't know much."

"There was a man with them?" continued Mary.

"Yes...a man we recently took into our employ," answered Jonas.

"A plump little man...he looks like...Santa Claus?" asked Mary.

"Yes, do you know him?"

Detective Phillips stepped forward when Mary put her head down.

"He came to our house yesterday. He spoke to Jared," said Mary.

"Did you hear what they said?" asked Phillips.

"No, we saw them through the window," Mary said as a tear rolled down her cheek. "Jared seemed upset."

"Had you ever seen the man before?" asked Phillips.

"Yes...at the mall. He seemed like such a good man," Mary said.

Stevens walked back into the room and placed a cup of coffee on the table next to Mary, who nodded appreciatively. A deep silence filled the room as all seemed to realize there really was no news of the two lost children.

Suddenly the silence was broken. All looked toward the hall, whence the sound of three loud thuds emanated and then was followed almost immediately by a piercing scream. As policemen ran toward the hall, Miss Grundick hurtled into the room, her eyes wide with shock.

"They're back..." she shouted. "Mr. Stone...it's Sarah.... She's back!"

Everyone jumped.

Nicholas, looking tired but calm, walked into the room with one arm around Sarah and the other around Jared. Both children were exhausted, faces smudged with tears, and clearly emotionally spent. No one moved for a moment as everyone was in total shock. Sarah then looked at her father and smiled broadly. She glanced up at Nicholas, who smiled and released her. Sarah ran to Jonas.

"Daddy."

Jonas opened his arms and caught her rush with a huge hug. Tears streamed down his face.

Jared looked around the room until his eyes landed on his mother.

"Mom?"

"Jared!" Mary shouted and ran to him.

They hugged warmly. Nicholas smiled at the scene as Amanda walked up to him with a hug. The relief in the room was palpable. Everyone spoke at once with smiles and tears until Detective Phillips recovered his composure and motioned to two officers to take Nicholas into custody. Amanda tried to hold on as the officers each took an arm and ushered Nicholas out of the room while Sarah and Jared were still occupied with their parents.

THE next morning Jonas sat with Sarah. She was dressed in her flannel nightgown and robe. He had an arm around her shoulder, and she snuggled contentedly against his body. "It's only an arraignment, Sarah. They will try to determine if he should be charged with a crime."

Sarah pulled away and looked quizzically at her father. "But he didn't do anything, Daddy."

"He took you and that boy without telling anyone."

"But he helped us...he taught us something very imp..." Sarah started before Jonas interrupted firmly.

"Sarah...he did a terrible thing. He shouldn't have taken you anywhere without telling me."

"But you wouldn't have let him take us, Daddy," Sarah said simply.

"I was so worried about you. We'll see what happens later, okay?" Jonas hugged his daughter close.

PENFORD County's courthouse was a stately structure of stone and parapets, gables and protrusions of various architectural periods. It was originally built in the late 1800s and had had several facelifts and renovations in the subsequent years. On this particular Christmas Eve morning, with the sun struggling to break through the gray overcast, it was the scene of much chaos.

News of Sarah Stone's abduction by the kindly old gentleman who had made such a wonderful impression at the shopping mall just a couple days earlier had spread fast. The streets were lined with the citizens of Penford, who wanted to see and hear, firsthand, the details of the latest tabloid event. Everyone hoped to be in one of the photos that would undoubtedly be on the cover of every major newspaper in the country. It wasn't every day that the daughter of one of America's wealthiest businessmen was kidnapped and then mysteriously returned, unharmed.

Fortunately for all those interested people, they were not disappointed. Cameras and reporters were everywhere.

Stevens brought the Stone automobile to a stop at the curb at the foot of a long, wide set of stairs in front of the courthouse. When Jonas and Sarah stepped out, they were immediately accosted by reporters, who fought their way past a police barricade. The next vehicle, an armored truck, arrived just as Sarah, Jonas, and Stevens were pushing their way up the stairs. Everyone turned at the truck's arrival. Although the vehicle's main occupant could have been delivered to the courthouse hours earlier by a back entrance, Penford's police chief was not above having his own picture in the papers. He made a show of exiting the passenger side of the truck, unlocking the back doors, and helping Nicholas to the ground with his hands cuffed behind his back.

Nicholas wore the same disheveled tuxedo from the party. He was tired and dirty, as if no one had provided him the opportunity to clean up during his day in custody. His usual smile was gone, replaced with a look of sadness as he searched the angry, jeering crowd for one friendly face. When his eyes finally fell upon Stevens, his friend's look was one of pleading, hoping that Nicholas had some kind of rational explanation for what had happened. He gave Nicholas an encouraging half-smile, and Nicholas's eyes moved to Sarah, who looked on in horror.

"What are they doing to him?" she asked her father before she tried to pull away and go to Nicholas's aid. She was restrained by Jonas. "Make them stop, Daddy. They're hurting him," she pleaded.

Reporters crowded Nicholas as the police hurried him up the steps. Mary Roberts and her children stood huddled together with the mothers of the other boys. At the top of the steps, Jared and his three friends were being held by police guards. They all looked on at the commotion surrounding Nicholas, when suddenly Sarah tore herself away from her father and yelled, "No!... Let him go!... He didn't do anything!" She ran to Nicholas. Jonas jumped to follow and shouted, "Sarah!"

Sarah reached Nicholas near the top of the stairs and grabbed him. "Let him go!" she shouted again.

Everyone stopped suddenly as Sarah latched onto and clung to Nicholas. A murmur of surprise that Sarah was trying so hard to protect the man who had kidnapped her raced through the crowd. One of the officers attempted to pull Sarah away from the prisoner. As Sarah struggled to hold on, Jared, with the best view of the scene, decided he had to act. He pulled out of the grasp of his own guard and ran to Nicholas and Sarah.

"Leave her alone!" the boy shouted. "She's telling the truth. He didn't do anything."

The thing that first shocked everyone about Jared's statement was that everyone heard it. Despite the shouts of ridicule directed at Nicholas, the clamor of an ever-shifting mob, the scraping, grinding, and operation of media equipment, and the general chaos of a large crowd, everyone heard Jared. It wasn't that his voice was so loud it carried the entire breadth of the crowd. Yet they all heard...or at least, they all perceived, in some way, what he had said and they fell silent.

Every single person stopped and looked at the boy; there existed a complete and utter silence.

Jared stopped at Nicholas's side. As an officer moved to grab him, Detective Phillips motioned him to stop. Nicholas's cuffs suddenly disappeared, and he smiled at the boy. He threw one free arm around Sarah, who smiled at Jared. The boy turned slowly to face the massive crowd.

"He didn't hurt us. He didn't do anything except show us...show us both that we were wrong." Jared spoke in a normal tone, and everyone heard every word. Most were bewildered by his words. "This is Christmas. All he was trying to do was show us what it's all about."

He glanced at Nicholas, whose smile encouraged him to continue. "It's about giving and not being selfish. It's not about gifts or money or things at all. All of that means nothing. It's about love. It's about giving our hearts and souls to others instead of always taking. Can't you see? This is a birthday...the birthday of the one who wants only that we love each other. That's the only gift any of us ever needs," Jared concluded.

"Where did he take you?" came a voice from the crowd.

Jared smiled and said, "You won't believe it. He took us to Bethlehem.... We saw the first Christmas. We saw the baby Jesus."

A shocked murmur crescendoed through the crowd when another voice shouted, "Who is this guy?"

Jared smiled again and bowed his head for a moment. His own sister shouted the answer, "He's Santa Claus."

Amanda ran to her brother and grabbed him in a hug as the boy smiled and repeated, "He's Santa Claus."

Jared and Amanda turned to Nicholas. He embraced them both.

"Thank you, my boy," he said.

Nicholas took Amanda's hand on the one side and Sarah's on the other while Jared took Amanda's other hand in his. Together they turned to the crowd.

"Please...all of you...listen to these children...and remember," said Nicholas. "They know the truth." He turned to his companions. "Remember well and remind all others." He then looked back out on the crowd. "Now, if you'll excuse me...this is Christmas Eve, and I have a lot of work to do." With an impish grin, he disappeared.

~ 14 ~

Sarah woke Christmas morning to a bright sun. On Christmases past, she was usually the first to rise, scurry downstairs, and demand that everyone watch as she opened the stacks of gifts under the tree. This Christmas was different. She expected nothing under the tree because she knew she'd already received her gift...a gift she would never forget for a day she would always remember.

As for the clothes, electronics, and other items she and Stevens had purchased at a time that seemed so long ago, she and Stevens had wrapped them and taken them to the Penford Children's Home the previous evening. They had left Mr. Johnson grateful again and with a promise that they would return Christmas day with her father in tow.

When Sarah did accompany her father downstairs, it was not to open gifts but rather to wish all in the house a Merry Christmas and to hurry Stevens and a Miss Grundick in their preparations to join Jonas and Sarah at Christmas morning services.

Outside, Stevens stepped lightly around the Stones' automobile. He opened each door and smiled as he awaited his passengers.

Jonas issued last minute instructions to the household staff for Christmas dinner preparations for the guests who would join them that evening. It was an unusual guest list by the Stones' traditional standards, but it was a guest list that would be magical, in Sarah's estimation. It included Sarah's new friends, Jared Roberts and his family.

When it was time to leave, Miss Grundick was standing in the foyer, smiling broadly. Gone was the pinched face and severe hairdo for which she had been known. Both were replaced by the Myra Grundick appearance and childish whimsy Nicholas had so fondly remembered.

"You look happy, Miss Grundick," Sarah said.

"I am, Sarah," she said and pointed into the library. "I think this is for you."

On a shelf of one of the bookcases stood a two-foot wide wooden base upon which was the most intricate and brightly colored wood-carved Nativity scene anyone had ever seen. Sarah could actually recognize Mary and Joseph in the features of the wood characters. Yet what was most moving was that in place of shepherds surrounding the baby Jesus, there knelt three other characters. One was a tuxedoed Santa Claus, the second was a young boy in a hooded sweatshirt, and the third was a young blond girl in a party dress. Protruding from beneath the nearest corner of the sculpture was a note. It read, "Merry Christmas, Sarah. Never Forget. Love, Nicholas."

Sarah hugged Miss Grundick tightly for the first time in her life, and together they were escorted out the door by Jonas Stone.

Jonas and his companions noticed immediately that Stevens was in animated conversation with Tom Burns. Behind Burns stood an unsmiling Mr. Kagumo and two of his business associates, all of Mokai, Ltd. They were dressed in dark suits that contrasted painfully with the brightness of the day.

Sarah's immediate reaction to the sight was hesitation, but Jonas didn't miss a beat.

"Ah, Tom...Mr. Kagumo, Merry Christmas!"

"Oh...yeah...Merry Christmas, Jonas," said Tom with some anxiety. He sidled up to Jonas, took his arm, and said, "Look, do you have a couple minutes?"

"It's Christmas, Tom. Shouldn't you be home with your family?"

When Tom didn't smile but looked furtively between Jonas and Kagumo, Jonas nodded to relieve Tom's pressure, and said, "What's the problem?"

"Can we go inside?" asked Tom.

"There's no need for that," said Jonas.

"Mr. Kagumo is leaving for Tokyo. We've got the deal, if we want it..." he whispered anxiously. "They got nervous when you said you could do the deal without them. We only need a few minutes."

Jonas looked at Burns and then at Mr. Kagumo, who stood stiffly with his hands clasped in front of himself and his chin aimed slightly up. Sarah looked sadly at her father, who didn't lose his smile.

"Look, Tom...Mr. Kagumo...I've thought a lot about this deal. I think your main office was correct, Mr. Kagumo. It won't work. I'm not interested in it anymore," Jonas said before taking Sarah's hand and escorting her to the car. It was painful for Jonas to let the deal go, yet he knew it was right. His business would survive nicely without it, and he had something more important to occupy his time...a daughter he loved. "You have a nice trip home, Mr. Kagumo. And you, Tom...have a great Christmas...Now, we've got a date at church and then some business of our own to attend."

Jonas and Sarah ran to the car with Miss Grundick, leaving a gawking Burns and Mr. Kagumo in their wake.

AMANDA stood in the hall, gripping her sisters' hands while the two younger girls strained to pull away. When she could hold them no longer, the twins broke free and ran to the Christmas tree, beneath which was a small treasure pile of brightly wrapped boxes. Amanda watched the girls, concerned that they would open gifts before the entire family was ready, but her concern disappeared when she noticed what else was near the tree—hidden, actually, around to the back.

As Mary arrived with Billie under one arm, Amanda's face spread into a huge smile. She whispered, "He brought it, Momma!"

Amidst the wrapped gifts was a shiny red two-wheel mountain bike with oversized tires, a water bottle, and a rack for anything Amanda might need to carry. Jared joined them and sported a wide smile. No longer was his face tight and angry...no longer were his eyes suspicious. He was at peace as he watched the younger kids tear into their gifts.

Mary turned to Jared, when there was a knock at the front door.

"I'll get it." Jared left the room as Mary smiled her thanks.

Standing before him was the second magnificent gift he was receiving this Christmas.

"Dad?" he whispered in shock.

Jared's father put a finger to his lips to shush his son. He reached in to hug the boy, who responded warmly before he led his dad into the living room, where Mary and the kids were concentrating on gifts.

"Merry Christmas, Mary," Joe Roberts said softly.

They all turned in shock at the sound of Joe's resonant voice. Amanda shouted, "Daddy!"

Joe was busy hugging all the kids as Mary stood, stunned. Tears welled up in her eyes and spilled over to her cheeks. "Joe, you're back," she whispered. "Oh, you're back." She ran to him and embraced him.

"I'm so sorry, Mary," Joe stammered. Mary pulled away slightly but held onto her husband before asking, "What happened, Joe?"

"I was scared, but... I had a dream," he responded hesitantly. "A little fat man...Santa Claus... told me everything would be all right. I cried my eyes out...I prayed."

He stared down at her, pleadingly, as tears filled his eyes. She smiled and leaned into another hug. *There would be time for answers and healing later,* she thought. *Joe's home.*

Jared stepped up and took them both in a hug as the younger kids became entangled at their feet.

AT the Penford Children's Home, Mr. Johnson stared open-mouthed at the check in his left hand. He tried not to blink for fear the check and the amount reflected on it would disappear. When he finally did look up at Jonas, he could say nothing. He simply grabbed Jonas's hand and shook it with a force and speed that rocked Jonas's entire body. Jonas smiled broadly and tried to withdraw his hand before his arm was pulled out of joint by Mr. Johnson's exuberance.

"This is only the beginning, Mr. Johnson," Jonas said when he was finally free. "We'll help you organize your fundraising campaign for the New Year."

Mr. Johnson could only gawk until tears came to his eyes. Jonas tried to keep talking so Mr. Johnson would not grab his hand again and do some real damage.

"My daughter told me about the wonderful work you were doing here and about the help you needed."

Mr. Johnson turned to Sarah. He tried to compose himself. "Thank you, Sarah," he said. Then his smile brightened even more. "It's lucky you came here today for another reason. Little Julia wanted to show you something."

Mr. Johnson motioned a teary-eyed nurse to bring Julia into the entry hall. After a short time, the little girl bounced into the hall, wearing Sarah's coat.

"Merry Christmas, Julia," said Sarah.

"Santa Claus came...and..." she paused and looked around anxiously, "um...look...Greggy."

Sarah and Stevens glanced quizzically at each other, when suddenly Greggy walked slowly into the room, a huge smile on his face. He clutched the Nativity globe Sarah had given him.

"Greggy...you're walking," Sarah whispered.

She ran to him and grabbed the little boy in an enormous bear hug. Jonas turned, bewildered, to Mr. Johnson.

"We woke this morning, and he was sitting on the edge of the bed. He hasn't been able to move in years," Mr. Johnson explained.

While continuing to hold the boy, Sarah glanced heavenward and whispered, "Thank you for this day."

AUTHOR'S AFTERWORD

On December 17, 1994, Loretta and I threw an eighth birthday party for our third daughter, Julia. Her birthday is December 24th, but, for obvious reasons, we usually had friend-birthday celebrations either a few days before or after the actual date.

On this particular birthday, we hosted eight seven- and eight-year-olds, in addition to Julia and two of our other three daughters, to dinner and cake at a raucous Hawaiian restaurant, a movie, and much hilarity. By that night, Loretta and I were exhausted although none of the girls showed any signs that their night was at an end. Nevertheless, within half an hour, we'd gotten the birthday celebrants into pajamas and gotten sleeping bags spread throughout our family room.

As I stood in front of the fireplace and the fire I had just kindled, surveying the chaos and only imagining what was yet to come, I had a vision of storytelling around a campfire. Since we hadn't done much camping in our lives, I hadn't

Back row, L to R: Hannah (mouth open), Kelly, Julia, Wendy, Santa, Kaitlin, Kendall. Front row, L to R: Autumn, Meg, Alex, Jeana.

had firsthand knowledge of such events. But I'd heard about them. I'd heard that a good rip-snorting fireside story was just the tonic for the roiling mass of eight-year-old exuberance that was about ready to explode before me. Although I had no hope it would actually work, I asked if they wanted to hear a Christmas story about some people who had actually seen Santa Claus. To my surprise and Loretta's obvious relief, they all shouted, "Yes!"

And so it was that *Mary's Son*, known only by me at the time under some long-forgotten title, was first heard. Loretta dimmed the lights. I sat on the fireplace's hearth, the flames warming my back, and told the story.

For nearly forty-five minutes, I sat before these kids gesticulating and shouting, whispering and conspiring, and ultimately performing as best I could. They were enthralled.

To this day, I don't know if all those girls believed the story. I know from parents' comments and from Julia herself that several did.

When one of the girls asked me if the story was really true, I responded softly, "I don't know for sure. But I know the people who were in the story. They told me these things happened, and I believe them."

Now you, dear reader, might ask me the same question, and my answer would be that some of the story is true, and some of the story is not. But whether it's true is not the real issue; for it is not the facts that matter but rather the message of love that comes from the truth of the birth of Jesus Christ. It is a love of all humankind...a love so genuine...so true...that if all people simply spend a few minutes every day pondering and living it, there would be a peace so profound in the world that pain, suffering, strife, and discord would cease to exist entirely.

I wish you Peace on Earth...Goodwill to All...and above all, I wish you *Merry Christmas* all your days.